Dancing with Mermaids

ALSO BY MILES GIBSON

The Sandman

Dancing with Mermaids

MILES GIBSON

E. P. DUTTON | NEW YORK

Copyright © 1985 by Miles Gibson
All rights reserved. Printed in the U.S.A.

Grateful acknowledgement is given for permission to reprint portions of
Speaking of Siva, translated by A. K. Ramanujan and published by Penguin
Classics (1973). The poem itself was written by Dēvera Dāsimayya, a tenth-
century Mudanūru poet.

First published in the United States in 1986 by
E. P. Dutton, a division of New American Library,
2 Park Avenue, New York, N.Y. 10016.

Library of Congress Catalog Number: 86-71532
ISBN: 0-525-24444-1

OBE

10 9 8 7 6 5 4 3 2 1

First American Edition

For Susan

Suppose you cut a tall bamboo in two;
make the bottom piece a woman,
the head piece a man;
rub them together
till they kindle:
tell me now,
the fire that's born,
is it male or female,
O Ramanatha?

Lyric no. 144
Speaking of Siva

Dancing
with
Mermaids

Chapter One

The River Sheep bubbles from a hole in Dorset and flows ten miles to the sea. In the beginning the river is a path of weeping stones but when it gathers strength it cuts a channel through the ancient chalk and the water is cold and deep. It pushes between hills, soft as the breasts of sleeping women, and floods the road at Drizzle. Beyond the village it rattles through a dark trench concealed by trees, roars into a field of nettles and spits at the cattle who come to drink. It is bright and wild and dangerous. And then, approaching the sea through a cleft in the cliffs, the river staggers, its courage fails and the ground opens up to swallow it again, leaving nothing but a swamp of poisonous mud. Two miles west of the Sheeps Mouth lies the town called Rams Horn. When the summer is hot, and a dry wind blows, the smell of the dead river invades the town and lingers on its narrow streets. The Sheep's ghost becomes a stink, an ooze, a yellow shadow, a broth of unspeakable secrets. It ferments in the blood of those who stand around on street corners and clouds the dreams of those who sleep with their heads beneath the sheets.

Rams Horn is a memory, a lost cause, a carnival of ghosts, an ark of half-forgotten dreams. Sometimes in summer, when the air sparkles with salt and gulls are dancing on the wind, the town seems to lean against the cliffs like a rusting ocean liner, thrown to shore by a storm. The decks are dark with faces, funnels belch sparks and the sound of engines can be heard as far as the mudflats. But when fog rolls in from the sea and smothers the streets, Rams Horn shrinks, phantoms walk the esplanade and the skeleton of Whelk Pier rattles its chains in the silence.

For a thousand years the town was a clutch of cottages, cut from earth and stone. The people were small and as ugly as gnomes. Brothers married sisters because the bible had not reached them: pilgrims on the road from Drizzle always drowned in the mud of the Sheep. The Rams Horn men smoked seaweed, cured in a mixture of rum and honey, while the women made shawls from the scales of fish. In fair weather they would take to the sea in shallow boats hunting for lobsters and dogfish. In foul weather they would hide in their hovels, watching the sea spray through the shutters while mussels cracked sweetly in driftwood fires.

In the summer of 1348 a French fishing boat full of corpses drifted into Melcombe Regis and the Black Death infested Dorset. Thousands perished, churches burned and towns fell empty. But Rams Horn was spared, since even the rats would not cross the river. Two hundred and forty years later, when Drake engaged the Spanish fleet, the people of Rams Horn stood on the top of the limestone cliffs and watched the smoke from the English cannon. But they could not guess who had won the day and received no news of the battle. They were a wild, forgotten tribe of men.

And then, at the beginning of the eighteenth century, a physician called Wilton Hunt, on a grand tour of England, suggested that mud from the Sheeps Mouth might cure fever, fainting and fits. Among the crumbling cottages he constructed a bath-house, shaped like a pyramid, and filled the tank with mud. When the news was carried to London the rich and foolish, forbidden to venture abroad by Napoleon, flocked to Rams Horn to wallow and gossip. They built a terrace overlooking the sea and paved the road from Drizzle. But five years later, when the mud began to poison them, they abandoned the town in a week and fled to wash themselves in the waters at Bath. The little Regency mansions with their marble floors and dainty iron balconies were deserted. The

Sheep flooded the road again and when the fishermen came down from the hills Wilton Hunt killed himself. They buried him beneath the pyramid sitting astride his favourite horse.

The town remained in disgrace until a Victorian parson called Hercules Shanks passed through Rams Horn while painting pages for *A Dictionary of Small Wild Flowers*. On the cliffs to the west of the town he stumbled upon some fossil bones. He collected a fragment of skull and several teeth and carried them back to London. For a time he used them as paperweights and then, grown tired of the novelty, gave the remains to a friend and forgot them. But Charles Darwin had published *The Origin of Species* and the parson's bones were soon exhibited as evidence of modern man rising from the ancient ape. The fossil fragments became a sensation. The size of the teeth suggested that early Rams Horn Man was a flesh-eating giant. A naked, pagan brute. The beast inspired a penny song sheet and correspondence in the *Tatler*.

The parson, who knew in his heart that God had created the world both perfect and complete on 23 October 4004BC, at nine o'clock in the morning, argued that the bones were those of a fossil horse. But London laughed at the very idea of Shanks's pony and the parson felt ridiculous. His sermons were ignored and his family was attacked in the street. He left England in 1865 and sailed for South Africa where he wrote *The Empire Dictionary of Tufted Grasses*. The book was never published and he died, mysteriously, in the Zulu War.

Rams Horn Man was nothing more than a prehistoric pig, but until the museum confessed its mistake, the town was guardian to one of the most important fossil beds in Britain. The Victorians opened Rams Horn to the world. They built a school, a factory and an ugly church. At the end of the century there was a post office and a motor-wagon that delivered dogfish to Drizzle.

A button millionaire built a small hotel overlooking the town and Hunt's pyramid stood in the garden, screened by an ornamental hedge. The hotel rooms were draped with silk and doubtful oils of sprawling nudes. In season there was dancing in the marble hall and laughter on candlelit lawns. But whenever mutton was served in the dining room Wilton Hunt would be seen, stiff as a corpse, riding down the central stairs on his hideous phantom horse.

After the Great War the town enjoyed a golden age. Men from factories in the North were sent to the sea for the sake of their health. The railways brought them in hundreds, along with their women, their dogs and children. Rams Horn learned to love these strangers with worn-out faces who sat all day and scratched in the sand. There were tea rooms and guest-houses, whelks, lobsters, oysters and Guinness. There were pleasure boats and telescopes, postcard views and sugar shrimps.

When it was hot there were deckchairs strung like flags in the shadow of the esplanade where old men collected to sleep and young girls ventured to peel off their stockings before they ran out to prance in the sea. Families trampled the beach from dawn until dusk and the great iron pier was ablaze with lanterns.

When it rained fat women with dimpled thighs drank Ovaltine in ice-cream parlours while children shrieked and squabbled like starlings. Young men nursed bottles of India pale as they swore at the rain through saloon bar windows and dashed, with their heads wrapped in newspaper, to the picture palace where, in the cat-calling, flea-bitten darkness, local girls with sunburnt noses watched Tarzan strangle rubber snakes. Later they would walk the girls along the beach and into the little amusement arcade which was dark as a cowshed and warmed by an ancient paraffin stove. They flirted and shouted and played the machines for trinkets, trifles or packets of Woodbines. There was a clockwork gypsy in a glass box who raised her hand and dispensed your fortune printed on a card for sixpence; an electric shock machine, a laughing policeman, and a brass kinetoscope with warnings to small boys that the views were forbidden, which never failed to make boys waste a penny for a glimpse of the huge and faded buttocks of the Sultan's Daughter as she flickered past their straining eyes. Then the rain lifted, the lanterns were lit on the dripping pier and Rams Horn steamed in the darkness.

For twenty years the town prospered. But after the Second

4

World War the summers turned cold, the Sheep stank and Rams Horn fell from fashion. Now the picture palace is a haunted shell. The laughing policeman burst into flames and reduced the amusement arcade to cinders. The ice-cream parlours were carried off one night in the teeth of a storm. The railway is closed. The legs of the pier are hairy with seaweed.

In the early morning the town stands invisible and remote. There is nothing in the world but the ghost of the moon and the sound of the sea grinding pebbles. Slowly, as the first few threads of light touch the hills, the houses take shape and the streets run black between them. The sun flies up from Sheeps Mouth and for a few moments the town is enchanted. The streets are luminous canals, the walls of houses glow like pearl, windowpanes flash, roof slates glitter and then, it is gone.

Cats stretch and sneeze in doorways. Milk crates clatter in the dairy yard. The butcher scatters sawdust and dreams of walrus meat as he prods the pork with sprigs of parsley. Mrs Reynolds appears in the high street, running on some secret errand, high heels clicking on the wet cobbles. Later Doctor Douglas leaves his surgery and walks the beach, stands to stare at Regent Terrace and dreams of finding Mrs Clancy sitting naked in his waiting room. Far out on the rocks boys throw stones at gulls and watch, in horrified delight, for Tom Crow to limp down from his lair in the cliffs, hair tangled and eyes full of stars.

Sometimes at night the inhabitants dream of the town, inventing all the narrow streets that lead down to the rolling, varicose sea. And sometimes, at dawn, the town remains as a dream, a whispering movement of water and shadows.

Chapter Two

One morning, while the sun still rolled among the chimney pots and the cobbles were steaming, three small boys appeared on the corner of Empire Road. Cruel as giants, cunning as goblins, they swaggered down the high street with their hands in their pockets and milk on their breath. They swore at Oswald Murdoch, the butcher, chased Tanner Atkins' cat down a drain, spat, with venom, on the baker's windows and fled up the street, past the post office, to the safety of the woods.

"We could keep her in the shed," shouted Smudger as they ran among the dark and dangerous trees. He was eleven years old and full of bright ideas. He looked at his companions, his blue eyes sparkling with excitement.

They ran towards the sunlight, jumped ditches, scrambled through brambles, skipped, somersaulted, wriggled and crawled until they reached the shelter of an old brick wall, perched high on a hill above the town.

"We'd have to bring her food sometimes," gasped Sickly, breathlessly. He stared down the hill towards the sea. From this height Rams Horn was no more than a puzzle of rooftops forced between the limestone cliffs.

"We could look at her whenever we wanted," said Vernie. He was twelve years old and already sprouting from his clothes. His feet had grown so big that his plimsolls had burst. When he walked he moved like a large, unhealthy stork. He poked a finger into his ear, looked at Smudger and grinned.

They clambered over the wall and fell together in a bed of tangled grass. The shed stood in the garden of an empty cottage. The cottage was derelict, the ceiling collapsed and the walls bulging, but the shed had survived. It was a tiny wooden bungalow built against the garden wall, half-hidden by bushes. They had discovered it many weeks ago, broken the padlock on the door and taken possession. They arranged themselves now on a pile of potato sacks and discussed the great plan.

"We could keep her in here and nobody would ever find out," said Vernie.

"Yes, but how are we going to catch her?" demanded Smudger impatiently.

"Well, we could say that Sickly had fallen down and broken his neck and then we'd bring her out and lock her up," suggested Vernie.

Sickly scratched and looked doubtful. He had a small face, pale and tender as a mushroom through living in the shadow of his nose, which was long and varnished with freckles. His ears were so flat that they might have been stitched down against the sides of his skull. His hair was ginger bristle. Smudger and Vernie didn't really like the look of him but he had been tolerated ever since they had met his mother.

Smudger's mother was fat as a porker and had a moustache. Vernie's mother wore curlers and kept her legs in bandages. But Sickly's mother was tall and beautiful and had slow, flirtatious eyes. She was the most exciting woman they had ever encountered and she had devastated their small, closed world of tame hedgehogs, gulls' nests and rollerskates. Vernie's fishing tackle was gathering cobwebs in a corner of his wardrobe. The model tramp steamer that Smudger had been building since Christmas, had been abandoned. She had overturned the natural order of things, invaded their dreams and fermented their blood. She had become the focus for all the sizzling fantasies that could be conjured up by their unripe lust. And the knowledge that Sickly didn't have a father made his mother seem especially vulnerable to their schemes of kidnap and assault.

Once she had invited them to tea and while she stood at the table to serve them Smudger had dropped his spoon on the floor and climbed down from the chair to retrieve it. He'd slipped beneath the table and there, breathless, on his hands and knees, in the twilight under the tablecloth, he had peered up her skirt. He had surfaced, bandy with excitement, and trembled so much that he'd almost fainted.

He looked around the shed and tried to imagine the woman made helpless on the floor, a toppled giantess, tied by the hands and feet, her skirt slashed to ribbons and her hair in her eyes. He tried to imagine her naked but it proved too much for him. He had never seen a naked woman.

"What happens if she starts struggling?" asked Vernie.

"We knock her down and tie her up," explained Smudger.

"We could get a mattress and a little table and a paraffin stove for when it gets cold at night."

"We could keep her in the shed forever," said Smudger who harboured a secret belief that she would finally fall in love and run away with him.

"The police would find out," said Sickly. The smell of the Sheep, sweet as molasses, sharp as acid drops, stung his nostrils and made him sneeze.

"You can tell 'em that she's gone on holiday," said Vernie fiercely.

"No," insisted Sickly. "They'll find out."

They glared at him. They suspected he was telling the truth. Vernie prised his tobacco tin from a crack in the floorboards and spent a long time trying to roll a cigarette. Smudger stared forlornly through the cracked window. For several minutes they sat silent and depressed.

"She has lovely tits," said Smudger finally.

"How do you know?" said Vernie. He struck a match, sucked and coughed and wiped his eyes.

"Sickly told me."

"Well?" said Vernie, turning on Sickly.

"I seen 'em," said Sickly smugly.

"How?" demanded Vernie.

"I seen her in the bath. I looked."

8

"Are they big?" said Vernie.

"Enormous," said Sickly, measuring the air with his hands.

"Does she have big nipples?" said Smudger.

"Big dark ones," said Sickly.

"Has she got a hairy snapper?" said Vernie gleefully.

"Yes," said Sickly.

"Is it curly?" said Smudger.

"I don't know – I can't remember," said Sickly.

"Of course it's curly," said Vernie impatiently. "Frank's big brother cut some hair off his girlfriend's snapper and kept it in an envelope. I saw it. Black and curly."

"Why did he keep it in an envelope?" said Sickly.

Vernie shrugged. "I suppose he liked to look at it."

"But we'd have to tie her up and everything," objected Vernie. He drew on the cigarette and spluttered smoke through the corner of his mouth. He felt rather queasy.

"Not if she was hypnotised," said Sickly. "I read about it. You hypnotise 'em and then they do anything you want 'em to do and when they wake up they don't remember anything about it."

"That's right," coughed Vernie. "If we could hypnotise her we could get her to come here and take all her clothes off and walk about stark naked and then we could get a real look at her and she wouldn't know anything about it."

"We could even sniff her snapper," said Smudger.

"Do you know how to do it?" said Sickly.

"No," said Smudger sadly.

"I've got a book somewhere that tells you," said Vernie. "I'll bring it with me tomorrow."

"Are you going to help?" said Smudger, leaning towards Sickly and glaring at him. Despite all their wild talk he wasn't convinced that Sickly would help them kidnap his own mother. It seemed too good to be true.

"Yes," said Sickly surprised.

"We'll cut your fingers off if you try and run away," threatened Smudger.

Sickly picked his nose thoughtfully. His shoes were loose and his dungarees were a size too big for him. He looked like

9

a jumble sale gnome. "I'll help," he said mildly. "I'll prove it. Tomorrow. I'll prove it."

The next afternoon they met in the shed and sat patiently while Vernie read aloud the principles of mesmerism from a tattered booklet stolen from his father's bookshelf. The booklet was called *Your Secret Power to Command*. The cover had a picture of a man in a turban pointing his finger at a beautiful woman. The woman had her eyes closed. The man had sparks leaping from his finger.

"You stare at 'em," said Vernie. "You stare at 'em and it sort of controls 'em until they fall into a trance. Then they'll do anything for you."

"I want to do it," whispered Sickly. His small white face seemed to glow with excitement. His ginger bristles stood erect. His eyes were alight.

"Why?" said Smudger.

"It's easy for me. She knows me. She won't suspect nothing," said Sickly.

"He's right," said Vernie.

"How do we know we can trust him?" said Smudger.

Sickly grinned. He rummaged in his pocket and pulled out a crumpled ball of pink cotton. He flourished it like a magician palming a flag. He was holding a pair of his mother's pants.

"I stole them," said Sickly proudly.

Smudger stared at the pants in disbelief. Vernie snatched hold of them, rubbed his face in them, chortled and fell back into the potato sacks. He wriggled his ears and smirked and rubbed his stomach and shrieked like a rooster. Smudger fought for them, gained possession and pulled them over his head. Vernie made little whimpering noises and screwed up his eyes in a pantomime of simulated ecstasy.

"She wore 'em," said Sickly.

"She wriggled her bum in them," croaked Vernie.

"Snappers," shouted Smudger with the pants pulled tight against his face. "Snappers." The word hissed, dark and delicious, through his teeth. His brain was a blazing bonfire. His hair crackled with lust.

They pranced and danced and wrestled until they fell

10

exhausted and the pants were no more than a frayed rag. Then they buried the precious fetish in the crack in the floorboards beside the tobacco tin.

Vernie presented Sickly with *Your Secret Power to Command*.

"I'll have to practise on someone," said Sickly.

"It won't work on me," said Vernie quickly.

"It doesn't hurt," said Sickly.

"You could practise on Old George," suggested Smudger.

"Does it work on dogs?" asked Vernie.

"It works on anything," said Sickly.

Old George was a large, yellow mongrel with torn ears, bad breath and a reputation for biting the hand that fed him. He lived under a wheelbarrow in Sickly's garden and pilfered from the neighbourhood dustbins. He was devoted to the boys and tried to follow them everywhere, snapping and snuffling at their heels.

Sickly agreed to the experiment and, a few days later, reported that he had Old George falling asleep at his command. The following morning they bundled the dog into a cricket bag, hauled him over the brick wall and pushed him into the shed. He crouched in a corner, growling and slobbering and glaring at the boys.

"He's vicious," said Vernie proudly as he watched Old George try to chew on his plimsolls.

"He hates the cricket bag," explained Sickly.

"Shall we feed him before we do him?" said Smudger helpfully. "I brought some biscuits."

"No," said Sickly. "I'll fix him."

They watched Sickly, on his hands and knees, crawl towards the puzzled mongrel. Old George growled softly and curled his lip. Sickly stared at him, his eyes popping and his long nose quivering with concentration. Old George stopped growling and cocked his head. Sickly continued to stare, without blinking or moving, for a very long time while Old George stood frozen with fascination. And then, very quietly, he trembled, toppled sideways into the sacks and closed his eyes. He began to snore.

"It works," whispered Smudger, horrified. They hadn't

really believed it. They had yearned for success, hoped and prayed that they might be given the magic, but they hadn't really believed it. And now anything was possible. They had found a key to unlock all the unspeakable mysteries of the world. They could stop life dead in its tracks and dance rings around it. They could walk on water, fly through the air, spit in the eye of the moon.

"Jesus," said Vernie, crawling over to the dog and peering at him. "Can he hear us talking?"

"Yes," said Sickly.

"Make him do something," said Smudger.

"I can't," said Sickly. "I tried to make him do things but he just lies there in a heap."

"We never taught him any tricks," said Vernie. "It's obvious. You can't expect him to turn into a genius just because he's been hypnotised."

"How long will he sleep?" said Smudger.

"Hours," said Sickly.

They sat in amazed silence like a group of pygmies confronted by the victim of the first stone axe. Old George lay at their feet with his eyes closed and his tongue peeping between his fangs. He looked dead.

"When can we do your mother?"

"Sunday," said Sickly. He had planned everything.

"Will she take all her clothes off and walk about stark naked or will she go like Old George?"

"It doesn't matter. When she goes into the trance she'll be helpless," explained Sickly.

"We can help ourselves."

"We can take off her dress."

"And pull her pants down."

"And look at her bum," screeched Smudger, flinging his arms around himself and rolling across the floor.

"And touch her tits and everything," roared Vernie.

Smudger frowned and sat up again, cobwebs in his hair. He looked around the shed. There was a problem. "How do we get her up here?" he said.

"We can do it at home," said Sickly.

"Now we can hypnotise her we can do it anywhere," said Vernie. "And she won't remember anything."

They emerged from the shed, scrambled over the garden wall and crept down the hill towards Rams Horn. Sickly walked beside Smudger, hands pushed deep in his dungarees, the sun gleaming on his nose. Vernie walked behind them, his long arms dangling, a plimsoll flapping in the warm dust. They walked in silence, drugged with excitement and fantastic dreams of Sickly's mother.

Chapter Three

Mrs Clancy threw back the bedroom curtains, tilted her face and let the sunlight warm her throat. It was almost noon and she had slept like a child. She stared down from Regent Terrace towards the empty esplanade and the sea. Above her head gulls screamed against the gathering cloud. Below, in the street, three small boys appeared, dragging a cricket bag. One of the boys was limping and his feet looked as if they were wrapped in dirty bandages. As the procession passed beneath the window the cricket bag began to struggle and the boys began to shout. Then the cricket bag exploded and a large yellow mongrel somersaulted into the gutter. The smallest boy, a pale dwarf with ginger bristles, tried to catch the dog by its ears. But the dog broke loose and scuttled away towards the beach. Mrs Clancy stood at the window and watched until the dog had vanished on the esplanade. A faint breeze, spiced with the smell of the Sheep, ruffled the lace of her nightgown and made her shudder. She snapped the window closed and turned back to her dressing-table.

She was a handsome woman with polished skin and a thick mane of hair, rinsed each month to the colour of chestnuts. She had the ripe bosom of a matron and the tight waist of a chorus girl. Her limbs were powerful, yet so slender at the ankle and wrist that her movements appeared very graceful and delicate. She had the muscular beauty of a Victorian courtesan and it was an illusion she liked to cultivate with the help of the most narcotic perfume and underwear of apricot silk. She took great pride in her appearance. The face she presented to the world was perfectly painted and, when she turned her back, the seams in her stockings were perfectly straight.

Despite the smell of rain in the street the sunlight was warm and strong. It filled the room, ignited the mirrors and glowed in the carpet. In one corner a cabinet filled with glass paperweights trapped the sunlight on its shelves in fat bubbles of brilliant colour.

Mrs Clancy glided to the dressing-table and finished her toilet. She applied a final coat of varnish to her mouth, polished her fingernails, preened her hair into smooth curls and when, at last, she could find no more work to be done, she began to move around the room, stroking the furniture and patting the pillows on the bed.

Finally, when everything in the room was to her complete satisfaction, she picked up her husband's shoes from beneath a chair and blew the dust from their toecaps.

Mrs Clancy was a widow. But she continued to sleep in the marriage bed and kept the window open at night for fear that her husband's spirit, flying home like a storm-tossed pigeon, might find itself locked out and roost elsewhere. To help the spirit recognise its earthly home she had preserved her husband's wardrobe of clothes and she liked to keep the doors of the wardrobe open and his favourite jacket hanging on the back of a chair. She admitted that the chances of him returning for his jacket or tobacco pouch after fifteen years were remote, but she liked to take precautions. He was more important to her in the other world than he had ever been on earth and she could not risk offending him.

She had lost her husband, Captain Turnpike Clancy, in Southampton Water and spent many years and a great deal of money looking for him. She had employed countless mediums and mystics in her search yet, despite their efforts to tease and cajole him to stretch out a phantom hand and deliver a message of comfort from beyond the grave, he had remained silent. Nothing could stir him. He had been so

15

stubborn in his resistance that Mrs Clancy had doubted sometimes that he was actually dead and thought he might be hiding somewhere in London with another name and another woman.

Finally something happened to change her fortune. She had, by this time, given up all hope of contacting her dead husband and turned for comfort to the collecting of small antiques. The money he had left behind she began to exchange for eccentric objects made of ivory, jade and glass.

One day, rooting through a corner of her favourite market, she had discovered a scrying crystal. She did not recognise it beneath its layer of grime but purchased it as a curiosity, took it home and scrubbed it with a soapy toothbrush. The cleaning revealed a heavy sphere of beryl, almost translucent in colour yet tinged with an acid green at its edge. It stood on a glass pedestal shaped like an eggcup and the base of the pedestal sat in a frame with tiny brass feet. It was altogether an impressive work of art.

She displayed the crystal ball on a circular dining table which she had covered in a cloth embroidered with elaborate hexagrams. And, remembering the rituals which she had often in the past paid small fortunes to observe, it was not long before she began to search for signs of her husband in the crystal.

After a little practice at deciphering the milky reflections she began to see vague images. She saw mountains sparkling with ice. She saw Atlantic harbours veiled in smoke. But still she saw nothing of her stubborn husband.

Disappointed and puzzled by the pictures, she sought the advice of her friends, gathered them around the table and told them of the things she had seen. After some prompting and a measure of strong tea, an old man who had been raised in Kashmir recognised the mountains as the Himalayas and immediately feared for the life of a nurse he had not seen for half a century.

"The old girl must be a hundred years old," he said, as he remembered himself as a boy in a valley of flowers.

"I hope there's nothing wrong," said Mrs Clancy.

"Nonsense," roared the old man. "I hope she burns in hell."

Next, a neighbour, who had lost her own husband in a storm at sea, recognised the harbour from which he had sailed and took it as a sign that she was to join him.

"It's a terrible gift," the neighbour had said as she peered into the crystal ball and saw nothing but fog. Two months later she fell under a train at Weymouth. Mrs Clancy's reputation as a scryer had been established.

Throughout her long career she had never once claimed to own any particular power of vision. The claims were made by those in Rams Horn who came for consultations. She merely squinted through the crystal, described whatever caught her eye and left it for others to make sense of it. The fact that she never failed to describe the secrets in someone's life surprised her as much as it surprised them.

When she tried to find a reason for her newly-discovered powers she always reached the same conclusion: her husband had risen at last from the grave and was using her to send messages from those around him in the ether to those around her in the living world. She turned her bedroom into a shrine and kept his photograph in a locket at her neck. She grew fat and she grew rich. In death, as in life, her husband had continued to provide.

She stood now in the bedroom shrine and gazed lovingly at the shoes she held in her hands. They were heavy brogues, stitched from thick slabs of chocolate brown leather and tipped on the heels with steel. Shoes built by hand to fit a man's feet like a pair of gloves. She placed them gently on the chair beside his wardrobe and tiptoed away.

On the table in the consulting room the scrying crystal was asleep beneath a purple shroud. The walls of the room, which was empty of furniture but for the table and the chairs that surrounded it, were lined with books and small antiques. The windows of the room were draped in heavy curtains upon which extravagant gold dragons chased their own tails in an elaborate embroidery. Mrs Clancy stood at the door and smiled. A little sunlight managed to squeeze through a crack in the curtains and glowed lovingly upon her face and arms as she sat down before the crystal globe.

Each month, when the moon was ripe, she held a magic circle. Candles were lit, the Tarot cards were spread on the cloth and the widow entertained her audience with a variety of parlour games. They were a small and satisfied group of spiritualists. There was Mrs Reynolds, who sometimes brought her daughter and helped to serve the sherry and biscuits. Mrs Dobson from Drizzle who had once been haunted by a lobster. Mr Hazlitt and Mr Vine.

Hazlitt and Vine were her two most devoted admirers. They were both small, dapper men and when they stood next to the magnificent Mrs Clancy she took on the appearance of a fat queen bee with an escort of drones. They fluttered and hissed at each other and sometimes drove her to distraction.

Mr Hazlitt was a florist. He owned a large shop in Dorchester and claimed to have succeeded in breeding a new strain of rose which he had christened the Hazlitt Beauty. There had been a great deal of controversy over this claim in rose-growing society and he was still fighting for the recognition he thought he deserved. He was a small man who wore satin waistcoats and a gold wristwatch. He was very careful about his appearance and was never seen without a rose pinned proudly to his collar. He wore the flower in the manner of an old soldier displaying his medal.

Mr Vine was a tailor. He had once cut cloth for the crowned heads of Europe but was now reduced to running repairs on the trouser seats of council clerks. His own clothes never gave an inch to passing fashions but were valued according to their volume and weight. His body never quite filled the suits he wore and for this reason he often gave the appearance of being slightly smaller and more crumpled than Hazlitt. But the two were perfectly matched in their devotion to the widow.

Their rivalry was constant and bitter. Hazlitt never lost an opportunity to load the woman's arms with great wreaths of scented blossoms. And he could afford sometimes to squander money on beads and bracelets. Vine, for his part, could not stretch to such expensive gestures. But he'd had the good fortune, on more than one occasion, to have actually been permitted to enter Mrs Clancy's bedroom and there ordered to take a tape measure to her voluptuousness and measure alterations for a dress or a coat.

When Hazlitt first heard the news he'd turned faint with rage. The thought of Vine alone with Mrs Clancy in her apricot silks was too much for him. The idea of the old rascal having leave to measure her most intimate parts made him choke on his own fury. He had interrogated Vine a thousand times about the matter. And Vine, true to his nature, managed to embroider his story with the most lavish and intricate details.

There were times when Mrs Clancy prayed for the florist and the tailor to enter into some unholy matrimony with each other and leave her in peace. She loved them as good and loyal friends but she could hardly be expected to entertain them in bed for their favours. She tried sometimes to imagine the pair of them stripped naked and placed mutely beside her in the sheets. Hazlitt with his large yellow eyes bleary with lust and asthma, his lacquered hair leaving snail's trails on the pillows. Vine, small and crumpled, his teeth left behind on the table and a thimble between his legs.

It felt cold in the consulting room. Mrs Clancy slipped off the shroud and gazed into the crystal, hoping to glimpse an ocean, a desert or a blurred and distant view of the Alps. But this morning she frowned and drew her nightgown tight against her throat. The sunlight shrank away through the chink in the curtains. Something had changed. Something was wrong.

The sphere looked bruised, the opalescent bubble had filled with curious worms of shadow. Mrs Clancy stared into the unfamiliar twilight and there, floating in the very centre of the crystal, as small as a maggot in an apple, something dark and something twisted stared at her with scarlet eyes.

She drew back in alarm. It must be a trick of the light, a speck of dust or something spun from her imagination. She blinked and wiped her face in her hands. Slowly, fearfully, she peeped again into the gloom of the crystal ball. Her scalp prickled with horror. The maggot had grown, swollen into a porridge of ugly, wriggling demons. Their faces were human but their bodies resembled toads. They clambered, one upon the other, biting and scratching as they searched for a crack in the magic sphere. She watched them, hypnotised with horror, as they called out to be released, their jaws open and their eyes burning. And as she watched she felt herself drawn down and sucked into their swirling dance. She felt herself shrinking as she drifted down to join them. Her trembling fingers reached out to touch the globe and in her trance it seemed as if it might be no more than a bubble of water waiting to be pricked by her fingernails. But·when at last her hand touched, the crystal cleared and the demons vanished in a cloud of milk.

She cried out in surprise and pulled away her hand. Shivers scampered beneath her nightgown. Had she been dreaming? Had she gone mad? She stroked her throat and glanced about the room, searching for other, unseen, horrors concealed in the curtains or woodwork. Her fingers felt frosted and she shivered again. But nothing in the room had been disturbed. A little clock chattered serenely among the bookshelves. The dragons continued to dance on the curtains. Beyond the window there were voices calling, a man coughed and a woman laughed. She had been dreaming.

When her courage returned she lifted the scrying crystal from its pedestal, weighed it suspiciously in her hand and held it up to her face. The beryl shone between her fingers, opalescent and unblemished. There were no ravens, toads or demons. There was nothing but a faint wrinkle of darkness floating in the depth of the fog. She pressed her face closer against the crystal, trying to make sense of the shadow. And there suddenly stood Beelzebub, naked and grinning, his arms thrown out and his penis stiff as a bayonet; Beelzebub, prince of the fallen Seraphim, calling Mrs Clancy to enter the crystal and kneel before him.

She screamed. She dropped the crystal ball. It hit the pedestal with a bang and rolled smoothly into the centre of the table. She kicked back her chair and struggled to escape. But the chair fell over in surprise, spearing her nightdress with one of its legs so that she screamed again and beat her thighs with her fist. As she tried to untangle herself a thin vapour began to spiral from the sphere and the room glowed with a strange and terrible miasma. She pressed herself against the wall, sobbing and hiding her face in her hands. When she dared to look between her fingers she saw Beelzebub squatting naked on the dining table. His skin was wet, his eyes were scarlet and he held a human skull in one hand. He thrust the skull at Mrs Clancy and grinned. When she covered her face from the sight of it he clasped his slender, shining penis and used it like a drumstick to beat a tattoo upon the skull.

A moment later Mrs Clancy fell in a faint on the floor.

Chapter Four

The moon hung, fat and full, over Rams Horn. It grew so ripe that it seemed to sink beneath its own weight, burned through the clouds and floated in the trembling sea. The deserts shone, the peaks of its mountains glittered, the craters were turned into brilliant lakes of light.

The sea shrank from the esplanade, Whelk Pier stood bleached as bones, marooned in a shallow waste of water, its hairy legs alive with crabs. Mrs Clancy cancelled her magic circle and locked the crystal ball away. Tom Crow sat out on the cliffs and waited for the stars to sing their song. Vernie and Smudger lay awake in their beds and stared at the moon as it sailed past their windows.

Sickly had told them that the full moon had a narcotic effect upon those hypnotised during its influence and the assault upon his mother had been planned for the following day. They couldn't eat and they wouldn't speak, their eyes rolled vacantly in their heads. They were driven half-mad with excitement.

Smudger lay in his bed and tried to imagine the beautiful somnambulist taking off her clothes at his word of command. But since he had never seen a naked woman he could not give wings to his flight of fancy. He concentrated and gathered together the full force of his erotic experience.

He had once seen the top of Polly's breasts. Polly was Mrs Reynolds' daughter, a sixteen-year-old savage with wild hair and wicked eyes. They had been digging for tidal worms in the puddles beneath the pier. Polly, grinning with horror, had been rooting out worms with her bare hands while he squatted on the sand, watching her work, with the bucket held between his knees. She had been wearing a thin summer dress and, if you watched and were patient, sometimes the sun would shine through it and reveal the shape of her legs which made him shiver and rippled the water in his bucket.

He remembered the wind whipping at his hair and the sand in his shoes. He remembered an old man walking past with a cod's head in his arms, dogs barking on the esplanade and the mocking seagulls. He had turned away for a moment and then, without warning, Polly was bending over the bucket, counting worms, and the front of her dress yawned open in his face. His heart began to creak with excitement. He had stared, yes, he had stared into the twilight where her breasts nested and seen the pale and mysterious bulge of them before she had pressed the dress shut with her hand. And then he had blushed and frowned and pretended not to have seen them. But he also closed his eyes to help burn the sight of them into his brain.

Yes. And there was more. He had seen the little beards of hair in Mrs Lapwing's armpits. He had poked his head through the hedge and watched her in the garden, hanging out washing. When it was hot she wore a pinafore so that when she stretched to reach the clothes line you could catch a glimpse of her armpits and in those soft, white purses she had curls of black hair. It was wonderful. Frank's brother had told them that you could tell everything from a woman's armpit. He said it was a sign of a hairy snapper. Yes. And he had seen Brenda Butler standing at her bedroom window wearing nothing but a shirt although it might have been her brother because it was dark and, anyway, you couldn't see much in the rain. And finally, while squatting under her table, he had memorised Sickly's mother from the ankles to the knees.

He lay in bed and tried to assemble a naked woman from the available fragments, but he could not fit the puzzle together. He turned his thoughts reluctantly to the dangerous art of hypnotism. What would happen if they couldn't bring Sickly's mother out of the trance? What would happen if something went wrong and they were discovered? He'd heard that they put you in prison if they caught you looking at nude women. He wrapped himself in his blanket and tried to sleep.

A few streets away Vernie Stringer lay in the dark and considered the enormous implications of their experiment. He knew about women. He had found a magazine called *Throb* in his father's wardrobe. It was frightening. He tried to imagine Sickly's mother in a variety of stimulating positions. He was going to get a good look at her and have a proper sniff around and everything. He might even cut a curl from her snapper and put it in a matchbox. They mustn't waste the opportunity. Jesus. It might never happen again. The complete stark naked surrender of Sickly's beautiful mother. Tomorrow he was going to uncover the secret that all the women in Rams Horn had contrived to conceal from him.

It was almost dawn before the conspirators fell asleep. The sea rolled home, embraced the pier and threw itself ashore, flecks of foam, toothpaste white, gleaming on the hissing shingle. Its breath was sour as vinegar. The waves were crowned with garlands of seaweed. The gulls gathered to shriek at Tom Crow climbing down from the cliffs with his milky, moonlit eyes.

Smudger went out to collect Vernie in the afternoon. Mrs Stringer answered the door and scowled suspiciously at the little visitor. Vernie was in the kitchen having trouble with his laces.

"Where are you going?" she demanded.

"Exploring," said Smudger. He blushed and scratched his ears.

"Keep from mischief," she warned, inspecting him from head to foot, and he blushed again. He thought women might have some special power that warned them of danger. When they sat on the beach, no matter how he contrived to look up their skirts, they always seemed to sense him and wrapped their arms protectively around their knees. Whenever he sat in the hedge to watch Mrs Lapwing hang out her washing she would always stop and look in his direction and, although he knew he was invisible in the darkness of the laurel, he would take fright and cover his face in his hands. They could sense danger to their persons. They knew when you were looking at them.

Vernie appeared at last wearing a brand new pair of plimsolls and trying to hide a paper bag beneath his shirt. His mother gave him a friendly slap across the head. He gasped and tumbled into the street.

"Behave yourselves!" she shouted.

"What have you got in the bag?" said Smudger when they were clear of the house.

"Equipment," whispered Vernie, glancing over his shoulder.

"I didn't bring anything," said Smudger in alarm. He had not thought they would require special equipment. What did they need for the occasion? Ropes? Knives? Rubber boots? He didn't want to think about it.

"I brought enough for everyone," said Vernie.

"What sort of equipment?" said Smudger, after they had turned into Lantern Street and were within sight of Sickly's garden.

"Scissors," said Vernie. "And a few matchboxes." He had an idea that he might be able to sell the relics stolen from Sickly's mother. A pinch of hair from her snapper would fetch a high price on the black market. He had collected half a dozen matchboxes and was determined to fill all of them with the little magic curls.

They crept into Sickly's garden. It was a long strip of rough lawn, flanked by flowerbeds. They tiptoed towards the house, following the shelter of the fence. When they passed Old George's wheelbarrow they were afraid that he would make a noise and raise the alarm. But when he saw them approach he snarled and slunk away through the pansies. It was perfect. They reached their hiding place and crouched in the bushes, waiting for Sickly to open the kitchen door.

"Do you think he'll do it?" whispered Vernie.

"He promised," said Smudger.

"If he doesn't, we'll murder him," muttered Vernie grimly.

25

"We could knock him out and take him back to the shed," Smudger suggested helpfully.

"And cover him with Bovril," added Vernie. "And get Old George to eat him." He squinted through the bushes and watched the mongrel asleep beneath his wheelbarrow. Old George had a weakness for Bovril.

When Sickly finally appeared he was wearing pyjamas.

"What's wrong?' said Vernie in alarm.

"I've got a cold – I'm supposed to be in bed," sniffed Sickly, wiping his nose on his sleeve. He smelt of sweat and Vapour Rub.

"Can you still do it?" said Smudger.

"Yes," said Sickly.

"And she won't know anything about it?" said Smudger.

"No," said Sickly.

"And we can do anything?" said Vernie, clasping the paper bag beneath his shirt.

"Yes," said Sickly. He led them into the kitchen and closed the door.

It was a small, untidy kitchen. The remains of a chicken filled a bowl on the table. The cupboards smelt of cabbages. There were toast crumbs on the floor.

"Where is she?" said Smudger, pulling leaves from his hair.

"She's having a bath," said Sickly.

"Are we going to do her in the bath?" Vernie asked him, horrified and delighted at the prospect.

"No, she might drown or something," said Sickly.

"Wait until she gets out," said Smudger.

"Yes, she'll go into her bedroom when she's finished. I'll do her in the bedroom," explained Sickly.

"Where shall we hide?" said Vernie. He saw himself hanging in her wardrobe like a vampire, his arms folded across his chest, waiting for the moment to strike.

"Wait here so she won't suspect nothing."

"Give us a signal when you've done it,' said Smudger.

"A whistle," said Vernie.

"Knock on the floor," said Smudger.

"I'll come and tell you," said Sickly.

"And we can go upstairs?" said Smudger.

"Yes."

"And have a proper look at her?" said Vernie.

"Yes."

"Can I have a drink of water?" said Smudger. His throat felt dry and his head hurt.

"Yes, but don't make a noise," said Sickly. The midget mesmerist turned and disappeared through the kitchen door. They heard the stairs creak as he crept towards his mother's bedroom.

Smudger helped himself to a cup of water and went to sit beneath the kitchen table, nursing the cup in his hands. Vernie squatted behind the washing machine and chewed his fingernails. In a few minutes they were going to explore every secret and forbidden pleasure that, for months, had tormented their dreams. They both felt sick.

"She's ready," said the hypnotist. He was standing at the kitchen door. His eyes were burning and a ghastly smile spread across his face.

The three boys went upstairs. Sickly gestured towards his mother's bedroom and Smudger pushed the door open. An intoxicating smell filled their nostrils, a blend of talcum, soap and scented bath water. The room was hot and dark. Heavy lace curtains filtered the sun at the window and spilled brilliant speckles of light across the carpet. Sickly's mother lay motionless on the bed, her hands curled together on her stomach and a pillow beneath her head. Her red hair was swept back from her face and feathered against her neck. She was wearing a white dressing-gown tied with a sash. Her bare feet pointed towards the door.

Despite the spell that Sickly had cast upon his mother she looked as powerful as a panther and the invaders were too timid to approach the bed. They stood pressed against the wardrobe and stared.

"Jesus, she looks dead," whispered Vernie. Her face looked smooth and ghostly pale. They had never seen her without make-up.

"No, she's breathing. She's in a trance," whispered Sickly.

"She's nude under her dressing-gown," whispered Smudger. He felt so lewd he wanted to scream. His blood fizzed like sherbet behind his eyes. His legs ached.

"Have a look," whispered Vernie.

"No, you're bigger than me," argued Smudger.

Vernie tiptoed to the bed. He was shivering with fright. He wiped his hands on his shirt, held his breath and took the hem of her dressing-gown between finger and thumb. He tried gently to tease the dressing-gown away from her legs.

"Can you see anything?" whispered Smudger.

"No," whispered Vernie. He was peering at the shadow between her knees.

"You'll have to take off her belt," whispered Smudger.

Vernie, standing on tiptoe, reached across the bed and pulled at the knotted sash. Sickly's mother opened her eyes and stared at him. She had not been hypnotised. She had been sleeping. She always slept in the afternoon. She stared in astonishment at her assailant.

"What are you doing?" she shouted. She sat up and pulled the dressing-gown around her legs.

"Just looking," squeaked Vernie.

He turned to Sickly for help and collided with Smudger who was already running across the carpet. Sickly had vanished. They pushed through the door and flew headlong down the stairs. Sickly's mother followed, shouting and swinging at them with her fists. She chased them through the kitchen and into the garden. The dressing-gown flew open and her big breasts bounced. But only Old George, safe beneath the wheelbarrow, turned his head to admire them. Smudger was screaming. Vernie had begun to wail.

Sickly, safe in his sickbed, listened with pleasure to the uproar in the garden below. He wriggled deeper beneath the sheets, closed his eyes and smiled.

Chapter Five

Doctor Douglas stood and stared along the esplanade. Two small figures were running towards him, caught between the shadow of the town and the glare of the sea. He watched as the figures approached, grew arms and legs and frightened faces. Then two pale gnomes ran past, their mouths open, their fists punching at invisible demons. At the end of the esplanade they turned, collided, recovered themselves and sprinted away down Regent Terrace.

A small, blue packet had fallen at the doctor's feet. He picked it up and held it lightly in the palm of his hand. It was an empty matchbox. The doctor examined it carefully, tapped it with his fingernails, opened it, closed it and then, disappointed, threw it into the sea. He watched it bobbing in the broth of seaweed that slopped against the esplanade wall.

He was a big man, tall as a thunder storm, with a handsome, crumpled face. He had been christened Edward Baron Douglas but was known in Rams Horn as the doctor and, by that name, ignored. Seven years ago he'd taken the surgery in Storks Yard and had his name engraved on the brass plate. In the beginning he was encouraged by the number of people who came to him with their problems and complaints. He wrote prescriptions as elaborate as love letters, offered his patients laxatives, purgatives and sedatives; lubricants, expectorants, embrocations and vaccinations. But as time passed the queue in the waiting room dwindled until, one morning, he found himself with an empty surgery.

He was surprised. He was suspicious. He waited for winter to bring leaking lungs and scarlet throats. But no one sought his advice. He waited for summer to bear a rash of blisters, burns and bites. But no one seemed to need his help. He began to believe that the little town must be spared any sickness worth serious medical attention. There were remote places in the world where people lived without fear of disease. The water disinfected them or some secret in the soil protected them. If he could find the secret of Rams Horn his name would appear in the *Lancet*. He was nearly fifty and after so many years of cutting corns and dressing boils he was glad of a chance to enhance his reputation.

So the doctor sat alone in Storks Yard and began to conduct an investigation of the soil, the vegetables and the local lobsters. After many weeks' work he was confident the answer lay in the river. The Sheep fascinated him. He tested the water and made delicate experiments upon stinking turds of mud. He read the pamphlets of Wilton Hunt and even paid his respects to the pyramid. His research was expensive and exhaustive. He found several parasitic worms in the mud and an ugly protozoan that he could not name, although he suspected it carried amoebic dysentery. But why the town should enjoy such rude and vigorous health continued to elude him.

He asked the old men of the town if they had ever drunk water drawn from the Sheep. But they shook their heads and looked perplexed. They didn't understand the question.

"You should ask Mrs Halibut," suggested one of the elders, a wrinkled sage in a woollen balaclava. During the war he had lost an ear in a threshing machine and wore the balaclava to protect his brains from the draught. "If there's anything strange in the water Mrs Halibut will know about it."

"She cured Tanner Atkins' varicose veins with maggot paste," said his companion, a large lizard with ginger whiskers. He speared the whiskers with a clay pipe and chewed smoke thoughtfully.

30

"Maggots?"

"Yes, but you have to soak them overnight in milk."

"That's nonsense," complained the doctor. "That's witch-craft."

"There's nothing more natural than maggots," said the one in the balaclava.

"She cured old Bedlow's liver with onions."

"That's right. And when I had the fever she helped me sweat it out with nettle brandy."

The doctor listened to these testimonials in complete astonishment. He began to suspect that his empty surgery owed more to Mrs Halibut than the magic properties of the Sheep.

He made other enquiries in the town. He remembered that Mrs Stringer kept her legs in bandages and when he asked about her health she confessed that she was under Mrs Halibut's supervision. He examined her legs and found a mild eczema that was caused by keeping her legs in bandages.

"I use Mrs Halibut's ointment night and morning," she said, staring proudly at her rash.

"Does it work?"

"Yes, I've been using it for years," she said as she rewrapped her legs. "And something for the pain," she added and brought him a large bottle of cloudy green liquid that smelt of juniper and cloves.

The more he learned about Mrs Halibut the less he liked it. She had long ago been accepted as the medical authority for Rams Horn, Drizzle and beyond. Her remedies might be harmless but some of the ailments they were supposed to cure could be dangerous. While the sick placed their trust in parsley he would never reach them with penicillin. A bad winter with an epidemic of influenza could kill everyone west of the Sheep.

Finally he resolved to confront Mrs Halibut and explain his fears. It was a warm morning in late April and beyond the town the ditches were crowded with cow-parsley. He walked as far as the Drizzle turning and then followed the old Jamaica Road until it narrowed into a cart track between dense black-thorn hedges full of fighting finches. He was hot and his shoes were peppered with dust by the time he reached the cottage.

He found himself staring at a handsome block of Purbeck stone planted in an undergrowth of shrubs. He kicked open the gate, pushed through the foaming wall of blossom and hammered on the cottage door. A bumble-bee sailed from the flowers and settled for a moment on his sleeve.

When Mrs Halibut appeared the doctor stepped back in surprise. He had been expecting a witch in a canvas apron, a rheumy druid or a mad mooncalf. He found, instead, a lean, middle-aged woman with green eyes and a halo of curly auburn hair.

"Good morning," he said, grinning like a fool. "Mrs Stringer let me look at her legs."

Mrs Halibut gave him a queer look and shrank back into the safety of the cottage.

"No, you don't understand," he explained. "My name is Doctor Douglas." And he slapped his pockets as if searching for his qualifications.

She hesitated, frowned at his shoes, and then invited him to follow her into the parlour. She was wearing a dark cotton caftan and, although it covered her from the throat to the ankles, he had an uncomfortable sense of her body moving beneath it, as if he had caught her preparing for bed. When she walked, her little feet kicking at the frayed hem, the caftan clung around her legs, her belly and the tips of her breasts. When she sat down it sank and shivered into the hollows of her body.

"Make yourself comfortable,' she said.

The room was small and filled with chintz. He perched on the edge of the sofa and spread his hands upon his knees. He stared at the knuckles for several moments, struggling to arrange his thoughts, while Mrs Halibut sat and watched him from her armchair beneath the window. The curly halo caught the light so that her face began to glow like a medieval Madonna.

"Don't say anything," she announced suddenly. "I think I know what's wrong."

The doctor felt relieved. He sighed and smiled and nodded

at Mrs Halibut. He should have known she would be sympathetic to his problem.

"Constipation," declared Mrs Halibut. "Try raw vegetables. Apples. Honey. And I'll make you up a rhubarb powder."

"No," protested the doctor, pulling at his collar. "I don't want a cure."

Mrs Halibut rolled her green eyes and tried to conceal her amusement. Nobody wanted to remain constipated. He really was a very strange man.

The doctor cleared his throat and tried to explain the reasons for his visit. He said that, as a child, he had been given a herbal cough mixture that was both soothing and delicious. He said that there were many wonderful cures to be found in plants. Science had refined these drugs, of course, but nonetheless there were still many secrets left in the forest. He said that diseases were mysterious in their origins and effects but appropriate treatment could always be developed in the laboratory. And then, when he could no longer conceal his complaint, he said that the good people of Rams Horn appeared to put all their trust in herbalism when they might obtain greater benefit from modern medicine. He would be obliged if she would recommend him to those who were obviously sick or in distress.

The doctor fell silent. He held his breath. He had expected her to be indignant but she sat quietly and retaliated with nothing more than a vague, disgusted stare that made him feel like a farting schoolboy.

"There are too many chemicals in modern medicines," she said at last. "They kill more than they cure."

"Everything is chemical. The elements of all creation are chemicals," the doctor explained.

"There are no chemicals in my medicines," said Mrs Halibut indignantly. "Grapes for the liver. Nuts for the heart. Bananas for the kidneys. It's what we call the healing hand of nature."

"But think of the damage you could inflict on someone with a serious condition," he pleaded.

33

"I don't give them anything dangerous."

"No, but they might need urgent medical attention. They could die without proper treatment."

"I give them proper treatment. Doctors used the natural methods for centuries. There's nothing wrong with it." She pouted and her lower lip grew as fat as a rose bud. Her face held the implacable innocence of a child. Her faith in the power of nettles, knit-bone and comfrey was complete. She had trained as a hairdresser but she preferred medicine.

"The serious conditions," he said again.

"Elderflower infusion for bronchitis. Yoghurt for heart failure. Mistletoe extract for cancers," replied Mrs Halibut gently.

"And how would you feel if someone you treated collapsed and died?" the doctor shouted. He didn't care what she gave her patients. She was free to feed them potting compost. But if they were sick they also needed efficient drugs. It wasn't a game. It was a question of life and death.

Mrs Halibut looked startled. "You can't kill someone with kindness," she said.

"It's a risk."

Mrs Halibut put her hands together and slowly knitted the fingers. "I would only regret that they hadn't reached me while they still had a chance of recovery," she said and offered him a sad but stubborn smile.

"But they're my responsibility," hissed the doctor.

"They're not your patients," she reminded him softly.

The doctor stared at her with his mouth open.

"You could live to be ninety if you took molasses in a little hot water to wash out your bowels at night," chided Mrs Halibut as she watched him struggle to his feet.

The doctor stood and stared at the floor, defeated. There was nothing to be done about it. He saw himself growing old in Storks Yard, sitting alone with the dusty drugs cabinet, a mad and feeble lunatic, his name scratched from the medical register, the victim of yoghurt and witchcraft.

"Thank you, I knew you'd understand the problem," he said, smiling vacantly and moving to the door.

"I'm trying to help you," explained Mrs Halibut. "Just

imagine – your surgery would be full every day of the week without all my work."

"Yes," sighed the doctor as he stumbled from the cottage. "Imagine it."

"You'd feel better without your constipation," she added sweetly as she watched him kicking through the shrubbery.

The following day the doctor went back to old Mrs Stringer and confiscated her bottle of herbal pain killer, hinting that it had originally been intended to clear thistles from lawns. Mrs Stringer, an enthusiastic hypochondriac, was thrilled and willingly surrendered her medicine in exchange for twenty sleeping tablets.

"Take two at night to send your legs to sleep," he said as he wrote the prescription. "Call into the surgery when you've finished them."

Later, when he analysed the dull, green liquid, he discovered Mrs Halibut's secret. The medicine he had stolen was super-market gin disguised with mashed herbs. His heart sank. Now he understood why her cures were so popular. She mixed cocktails of folklore and spirits.

He stood on the esplanade and watched the empty matchbox swimming in circles. He prayed for a plague. He wanted to show the town the power of his own medicine. He needed a surgery full of sweating, frightened faces; raw throats and swollen glands. How could he demonstrate his superior skills unless the people of Rams Horn were prepared to suffer for the sake of their health? He wasn't asking for the moon. Mrs Halibut was welcome to treat all the warts and whitlows. A small group of appreciative patients with interesting complaints would be enough to satisfy him. He was lonely.

And then, despite himself, he thought again of Mrs Clancy sitting in the surgery chair while he held her head between his hands and watched as she teased him with her tongue. She had consulted him briefly one morning for an antiseptic gargle. It was nothing serious. He might have written the prescription without giving her an examination. But it was raining outside, the waiting room was empty and Mrs Clancy was a handsome woman.

"I think we should have a look at you," he said casually, kneeling down beside her chair. She was wearing a white silk shirt and a string of little amber beads. He unpicked the button on her collar and placed his hand against the warmth of her throat. The beads clattered. Perfume came whispering from her breasts.

"Is it sore?" he said.

"Yes," she whispered and closed her eyes.

He stood up and walked behind the chair, holding her head in his hands, tilting her face and letting the heavy, polished hair spill through his cradle of fingers.

"Show me your tongue," he said.

Her lips parted to reveal her teeth and she let him peep at the slender tip of her glistening tongue.

"Open your mouth," he whispered.

She opened her mouth and flicked out the stiff and trembling blade. Dear God, he bent towards her face and almost fainted with the force of his desire. He wanted to fall upon her mouth, clasp her tongue between his teeth and devour it. He wanted to throw her against the floor, snap all her buttons and roll her buttocks in his hands. It was madness. He scribbled the prescription with trembling fingers. It was bad enough that Rams Horn ignored him. He wasn't going to help his reputation by threatening to attack the few women who still came to him for advice. He pushed the prescription into her hand and hurried her through the door.

But he couldn't forget Mrs Clancy. Since that first encounter she had tormented his days and filled his nights with sorrow. He had dreams in which she fell down stairs and was carried senseless into Storks Yard upon a litter of straw, her hair loose and her breasts torn free from their harness. In the dreams he would force the kiss of life upon her mouth until she struggled, moaned, and he woke up gasping for breath with his face buried into the pillow.

He turned and stared across at Regent Terrace, squinting up at the windows where Mrs Clancy moved, unseen, behind the half-drawn curtains. The sea roared against the esplanade. The matchbox sank through the black and tangled seaweed.

Chapter Six

Mrs Clancy lay in bed and refused to speak to a single soul, living or dead. With her head supported by a mountain of herb pillows she languished, with her eyes lightly closed and her arms crossed over her broad bosom, trying to make sense of the devils she had seen in the glass. She had reached the conclusion that her late husband was responsible for the dancing Beelzebub but why he had chosen to announce himself by throwing her into a fright remained a mystery. For years Captain Turnpike Clancy had eluded the finest clairvoyants in London, her own scrying crystal had revealed no trace of him, and now he was mysteriously close at hand, reaching out to her with some diabolic warning that she could not understand. She had done nothing to upset or disappoint him. There seemed no sense in such an ugly manifestation when he could have chosen to speak to her through the tea leaves or Tarot cards.

She had met the Captain at a summer dance and she'd been overwhelmed by his experience and charm. She was a village girl, sheltered and painfully innocent. He could speak French and German and dance the tango. He gambled at cards and drank pink gins. His smile was quick and his legs were strong. Eager to capture a virgin he had married her the following spring and taken her to India for the honeymoon.

"Nothing shall ever separate us," vowed Mrs Clancy the bride.

"We'll be together forever," smiled the beautiful young officer and kissed her neck.

She closed her eyes and repeated the words. Together forever. And she knew then that they would love each other to death, into the grave and beyond.

She remembered how they had stood together on a hotel verandah sipping cocktails at dusk and listening to the peacocks scream. He'd smoked a cigar and gazed silently out across the desert, his face dark and suddenly forbidding and remote. When he turned to her again and drew the shawl around her shoulders, she glimpsed a violence in his eyes that disturbed her, making her tremble and blush. The walls of their room were hung with tapestries and rugs. Incense smouldered in a brass dish. The bed was veiled. His body was cool. All night she lay in his arms, while the blades of the fan whispered softly in the spiced darkness.

She had been ravished and plundered by that hairy giant of a man in every hotel in every large town between the Punjab and Madras.

At an ancient hotel in Manali, on a balcony overlooking the Kulu Valley, scented by the pine forest, in full view of the snow-clad Himalayas, he had stolen up behind her, torn open her skirt and fondled her belly.

In the Rambagh Palace, the sugar-spun castle that stands above Jaipur, they had anointed each other with jasmine oil and wrestled together, slippery as salmon, on the cold marble floor.

Locked in a room in Hyderabad, he had attacked her with fruit of every description, mango, guava and green banana, and could not be satisfied until she lay bruised and exhausted, the juices seeping from her body and her skin glistening with warm fruit pulp. Later, waking from her stupor, she'd discovered the fragrant syrup had dried and glued her against the bed linen so that she'd had hysterics and had needed to soak herself free in the bath.

The memory of the Captain made her ache with the weight of the years since their separation. Only her conviction that he could be retrieved from the grave had prevented her from taking her own life and flying to him in those first, anguished months after his death. She raised a hand weakly from her breast and took up a glass beside the bed, sipping at a little peppermint and Perrier for comfort.

Despite her lost love she had been spared many of the pains and disappointments of life. She might have starved on a widow's pension, but sorrow itself had been the catalyst which had revealed the new and unexpected talents from which she now derived considerable financial comfort. Her health might have failed at any time during her period of mourning, but the years had matured and ripened her body where they might have shrunk and broken it. There had been opportunities for new romance in the past and, no doubt, there would be men who admired her in the future. But no one, she reminded herself, could replace the Captain. She remained faithful to him even in sleep, for when her dreams forced open her legs and sent her mouth fluttering it was the Captain she saw in her passion.

She languished for nearly a week and not until Mrs Reynolds paid a visit could she bring herself to pick up a dressing-gown and venture from the safety of her bed.

"We were worried when you cancelled the magic circle. We thought you might be sick," crooned Mrs Reynolds as they embraced at the door. She was wearing a striped blazer and a big linen skirt, white stockings and shoes. The previous Christmas, inspired by brandy, she had cropped her long hair to bristle and kept the stubble stained a ferocious copper colour that seemed to smoulder now against the delicate, white face as she swept into the room. Her ears, so pink and naked without the shelter of her hair, had been dressed with silver barnacles. She turned and offered Mrs Clancy a dazzling smile, threw herself into the sofa and squirmed comfortably.

"What happened?" she asked.

"I haven't been sick," said Mrs Clancy, sitting down beside her in a nest of silk cushions. "At least, it was nothing physical."

"Can you tell me about it?"

"It's not easy to explain," said Mrs Clancy.

"I understand. Believe me, I won't breathe a word," whispered Mrs Reynolds, like a good matron. She was younger than Mrs Clancy, although her exact age was a mystery. Mrs Reynolds enjoyed mysteries.

"We've had a visitor."

"Yes?" Mrs Reynolds blinked her soft grey eyes. She owned a guest house on the esplanade. She knew about visitors. They usually slept in her bed.

"A visitor from beyond," said Mrs Clancy, raising a finger in the direction of the ceiling.

"Yes?" Mrs Reynolds blinked again. She had supposed clairvoyants were always entertaining guests from the grave.

Mrs Clancy shook her head. "It was terrible," she confessed miserably as her fingers prodded and poked at the cushions. Her voice was so small that Mrs Reynolds found herself leaning forward, straining to catch the words. "I thought it was going to drag me away. I must have fainted. It was sitting there, on the table, grinning at me. Horrible."

"Good Heavens! What was it?" Mrs Reynolds began to sense that something was wrong. She had seen Mrs Clancy pluck phantoms from candle flames, catch messages from passing corpses and talk in tongues; but she had never seen her look so frightened and haunted. There were shadows beneath her eyes and her whole face seemed to be shrinking, as if her body had been invaded by some unspeakable horror that was sucking at her soul. What had she endured that was so dreadful it could frighten her almost to death?

"It came from the crystal," Mrs Clancy said at last.

"What shape did it take? Was it big? Was it horrible?"

"Dreadful," said Mrs Clancy. She closed her eyes for a moment and there again was Beelzebub, squatting naked on her table and grinning as he beat on the skull with his beautiful, polished drumstick. "I couldn't describe it," she gasped, fluttering her eyes to shake out the sight.

"Oh, my poor friend," sighed Mrs Reynolds, glad to be spared a description of whatever loathsome monster had been conjured from the cemetery clay.

"I'm afraid it's a warning from the spirit world," said Mrs Clancy, staring at nothing. "Something is going to happen. Something terrible." Her voice faded away. She was surprised to find herself on the brink of tears and, knowing that her admirers believed she rubbed shoulders with demons every day of the week, she tossed her magnificent mane to hide her face in her hair.

"But why should anyone want to hurt you?"

Mrs Clancy brushed the tears away with her hair and gave Mrs Reynolds a long, sad smile. "It's wrong to disturb the dead. I've always tried to ignore the risk. But Satan could snatch me away with a snap of his fingers."

"And the rest of the circle?"

"I don't know. But we shouldn't hold another meeting until the spirit world is at peace."

"You mean we could all be in some kind of danger?" whispered Mrs Reynolds nervously.

"I can't tell you. Perhaps the town itself is in danger. Have you noticed anything strange happening out there in the last few days?"

"No." Mrs Reynolds frowned and scratched her neck thoughtfully.

"Ah." Mrs Clancy nodded, as if nothing meant everything.

"Oh, Mercy Peters was attacked by some small boys – in her own bedroom if you please. But there was no harm done. She seemed to find it rather amusing," said Mrs Reynolds.

"Wasn't she frightened?" gasped Mrs Clancy.

"Good gracious, she isn't frightened of anything."

"But didn't they try anything?" breathed Mrs Clancy in a shocked whisper.

"No, they were just standing there, staring at her while she was resting on the bed. She closed her eyes for half an hour and when she woke up they were standing there, peering at her with their eyes as big as saucers. They must have got into the house while she was having a bath."

"What did they want?"

"They said they were just looking," chuckled Mrs Reynolds and her grey eyes crinkled with pleasure.

"Did she recognise them?"

"Well, she has her suspicions," smiled Mrs Reynolds. "But she says all small boys look the same."

"Isn't Mercy Peters the woman with the strange-looking child?"

"Yes, but he wasn't involved," explained Mrs Reynolds. "He was in bed with a cold and he slept through the whole affair."

"Women living alone are always at risk," declared Mrs Clancy testing the knot on her dressing-gown. There were times when she couldn't even answer the telephone for fear of some diseased madman whispering filthy suggestions in her ear.

"I told her to buy a dog," said Mrs Reynolds with a shrug of her shoulders. "But she said she has one in the garden."

"It doesn't stop them. Some of them would think nothing of killing a dog."

"They were only children," protested Mrs Reynolds.

"That's what I mean – they get younger – it's so sinister."

"You think it has something to do with what happened to you?" said Mrs Reynolds, reaching out to touch her friend's hand.

"No," sighed Mrs Clancy. A woman could defend herself against the dandiprats but who knew what horrible appetites the devil might satisfy upon a fainting woman? When she had recovered her senses it had been dark outside, her nightdress was torn and the scrying crystal was empty. She had been surprised to find herself still in the land of the living. Yes, glad to be alive and unmarked no matter what lewd and disgusting rituals had been performed upon her sleeping body. But she knew it wasn't finished. She had helped a jinnee from its bottle and, wherever the monster was hiding, it was only waiting to change shape and strike again. She wrapped herself in her arms and shivered.

"Is there anything I can do for you?" asked Mrs Reynolds kindly.

"You could pour us both a good, strong drink," suggested Mrs Clancy.

Mrs Reynolds stood up, walked over to the little Turkish cabinet and searched through the spirits for a bottle of brandy. She felt encouraged. Whenever they had shared troubles in the past they had also shared their brandy. It had fired them, inspired them and given them strength. When the winters were so long and lonely that they thought they might leap from Whelk Pier and drown themselves, they had drowned their sorrows, instead, in brandy. When Polly had nearly died from summer fever Mrs Clancy had arrived at their door with the brandy bottle and had sat all night beside the bed. Mrs Reynolds had not forgotten. And now, please God, the brandy would work to burn out the ghosts that were haunting them.

"Isn't that the doctor down on the esplanade?" asked Mrs Reynolds as they stood at the window, sipping brandy and staring mournfully out to sea.

"We don't need a doctor," said Mrs Clancy with a toss of her head. "We need a priest."

Chapter Seven

The doctor tried to forget Mrs Clancy. He set to work on a long and controversial paper attacking the placebo effect of herbal medicine. He learned to build bookshelves and painted the waiting room green. But it wasn't enough. At night, when he could find no work to occupy him, he would go out alone, walk along the beach, stop at the Dolphin to sit for an hour with a glass of beer, and stroll reluctantly back to Storks Yard. His loneliness grew with the stealth of a tumour.

The landlord of the Dolphin was an old wrestler called Big Lily White. He was a short man with a foul mouth concealed beneath a large moustache. He liked to brag of his career as the Masked Terror. But no one listened. He had lost his hair and his muscle had melted to fat.

Lily White's favourite story was his assault upon the world mid-heavyweight championship. The belt had been held at the time by Cocker Harris of the notorious Bedlam Brothers. Cocker Harris was vicious but Lily White was cunning. They spent the first round of the fight threatening each other and shouting at the audience. In the second round Lily White gave Harris several hard postings to knock the air out of him and then, with no more than a neat leg dive, rolled him into a perfect folding press for the first pinfall. Harris turned nasty in the third, converted a crutch hold into a punishing pile driver and followed it down with a kick in the face. But Lily White retaliated in the fourth with the surreptitious employment of his fists until Harris began to grovel. Big Lily White maintained he would have won the belt in the fifth, if he hadn't been trampled and thrown through the ropes. He broke his nose and several teeth.

When Big Lily White retired he bought the Dolphin and learned to wrestle with barrels of beer. He missed the old days. Sometimes he would practise the head twist and strangle on old Tanner Atkins who helped to wash glasses. Tanner adored him.

The landlord disliked the doctor. He was of the opinion that it wasn't healthy for one man to want to worm another and he viewed the doctor with loathing.

"I once went to a doctor," Big Lily White confessed to Tanner one evening while the doctor was sitting at a table, nursing a glass of Badger beer.

"Is that right?" said Tanner Atkins.

"It was after my last big fight," said the landlord, blowing through his moustache. "I got headaches. Terrible headaches. I thought I might be having a turn. So I went to a doctor."

"Is that right?" said Tanner Atkins.

Big Lily White glared across the length of the bar and slapped a puddle of beer with his hand. He sniffed his fingers and wiped the hand on his apron. "I just wanted something for the pain," he grumbled. "Anyway, this so-called doctor tried to make me see a psychiatrist. He must have thought I was mental if he thought I was going to see a psychiatrist. Once they get hold of you they never let you escape. A headache doesn't mean you're mental, does it?"

"Plenty of people get headaches," said Tanner Atkins, nodding his head and giving the landlord a twisted grin.

"Plenty of people with headaches walking around the place all the time," grunted Big Lily White. The two men leaned on the bar and watched the doctor in silence for a few moments.

"It's some of these doctors who should have their brains examined, in my opinion," continued Big Lily White with a shudder.

"Is that right?" said Tanner Atkins.

"Well, it's obvious when you think about it," he growled.

45

"They sit in their fat leather chairs all day and get young women to undress and parade about the room and then they fondle them and everything and most of the time there's nothing wrong with them. So they talk a lot of fancy language and scribble of lot of nonsense and the women don't know the difference."

"They probably don't even know the difference," grinned Tanner Atkins.

"I know these so-called doctors are meant to be special from ordinary people. But I don't believe it," grunted the landlord, pulling himself up to his full height.

"Is that right?" said Tanner Atkins.

"How would you feel if lovely young girls came to your house and asked you to examine them?" asked Big Lily White as he cracked the cap from a bottle of cider. "I mean, they actually stand there in the complete nude and ask for it. You never stop feeling human, do you? You never stop having thoughts. If you ask me, it's the doctors who are mental. It gives me the willies just thinking about it." He sniffed his fingers and wrapped them carefully in his apron.

Chapter Eight

The stranger appeared late in the afternoon. Charlie Bloater was the first to see him. Charlie lived aboard a boat in a cabbage patch on the Upton Gabriel Road. He was a small man with chipped and tattered hands. His eyes were barely blue and his soft, grey hair curled out of his skull like smoke. He gave off a rich, vegetable smell and wore a set of cheap teeth that clicked when he opened and closed his mouth. He had lived so long in the cabbage patch that he'd grown to resemble a scarecrow. His legs were stiff with arthritis and he stuffed his boots with straw.

Charlie had lived all his life among cabbages but he dreamed he was lost at sea. As a small boy, watching his father battle with root fly, weevil and moth, he would stand waist-deep in the green and crinkled undergrowth and dream he was sailing Atlantic waters, adrift on the dark Sargasso. In the evenings, while his father slept by the cottage fire, Charlie learned to make ships in bottles: smacks, cutters and men o' war, fully rigged with darning thread. He loved and feared the open seas. As a young man he had planned to sail from Rams Horn as far as the Caribbean, find the Panama Canal and reach the Pacific. He would anchor off Fiji, Samoa and Tonga and when he grew tired of the islands, he would follow the humpbacked whales into the Southern Ocean. He drew charts and made maps for the voyage. But his father died and left him the cottage and cabbage patch.

For a time it seemed that Charlie's dreams had run aground. His father had managed to slip away while he still owed money to all the shopkeepers in Rams Horn. The cottage roof leaked, the cabbage crawled with caterpillar and the old man's burial took his savings. After the funeral Charlie went down into town, stayed drunk for a week and slept on the beach. Then he went back to the cottage on the Upton Gabriel Road. He worked all day stuffing the rotten thatch with bracken and he worked all night washing the cabbage with vinegar and milk. And while he worked a great plan was taking shape in his head. At first the plan was no more than a dream to comfort him while he struggled to pay his father's debts. But soon it devoured him.

The following spring he began to build a boat in the cottage. It was a boat of his own design, a big-bellied, clinker-built ark with a fat stern and a high bridge. It took him three years to build his boat and when it was finished it filled the cottage from floor to ceiling. During the last few weeks of its construction he had to sleep beneath the hull, on the kitchen floor, in a pile of wood shavings. And then, since he no longer wanted the cottage, he knocked down the walls, burned the thatch and lived in the boat on his cabbage patch sea. He fitted the cabin with a table, a stove and his charts of the coral islands. He washed from a bucket and slept in a hammock.

During the winter when the wind was sharp with salt and the rain screamed through the trees, he liked to lock himself below deck and listen to the force of the storm above him. When summer nights becalmed the boat he would sleep above deck, rolled naked in the hammock, with his face exposed to the stars.

Charlie was sitting on board, smoking a pipe, when the stranger came walking into view of his shipshape world. It was a hot and breathless afternoon. The heat had flattened the hedgerow and scorched the rump of the hill. The boat timbers creaked. The cabbages stank. The air was spangled with pollen. The stranger appeared as a long, black shadow in the dust of the white gravel road. He wore a black suit and thick black boots. He held a black suitcase in his black hands and, as he drew level with the boat, he turned a black face towards the cabbage patch.

"Ahoy!" he roared, tilting his head and staring up at old Charlie.

"Ahoy!" shouted Charlie from the safety of the boat and stared at the stranger in amazement. He had read about men from the Caribbean but he had never seen one alive and walking on the Upton Gabriel Road. He had heard that some of them were cannibals.

"I'm looking for a place to stay," said the stranger, grinning and showing Charlie his teeth.

"Good luck," shouted Charlie and waved goodbye.

"Can you direct me?"

Charlie clambered down from the boat and stood, reluctantly, on the warm earth. "Where have you come from?" he asked, staring at the intruder with a frightened grin.

"Southampton," said the stranger. "I came ashore last week. Cape Town. Libreville. Tangier. Southampton."

"That's a long way," said Charlie, who had never been to Southampton, and he scratched his head with the stem of his pipe.

"Now I'm looking around," said the sailor and laid his suitcase gently among the cabbages. He was a giant of a man. He strained the seams of his threadbare jacket and stretched the leather of his boots. When he turned to glance at the empty road his shadow covered Charlie in darkness.

"You'll be going to Rams Horn," said Charlie nervously, as he watched the sailor stroll away through the cabbages to get a better view of the boat.

"Does it have a hotel?"

"The hotel is closed," confessed Charlie, following in the giant's footsteps. In one corner of the field he had planted radishes for Mrs Halibut. She took as many bunches as he could grow and paid him in bottles of thick and potent vegetable wine which he drank to soothe his arthritis.

"She's a fine boat," said the sailor, trampling through the radish bed.

"Small berth," said Charlie, shaking his head.

"Broad beam," argued the sailor and stretched out his arms as if measuring himself for the cabin.

Charlie stared mournfully at the broken radish leaves clinging to the sailor's boots. "There's a woman who keeps rooms," he said at last.

"Are the rooms clean?" asked the sailor suspiciously.

"Spotless," said Charlie, clicking his teeth.

"And the woman?"

"A Christian."

The sailor rolled his eyes and stared at the sky. "Where can I find this woman?" he said, peering thoughtfully at Charlie.

"Walk down to the sea at Rams Horn. She keeps a house on the esplanade. A blue house with a red door," said Charlie, nodding towards the town. He had heard Mrs Reynolds rented rooms. He didn't know much about it but he thought she served breakfast and a hot supper for those with an appetite.

"Will there be any trouble?" said the sailor.

"No trouble," said Charlie, looking perplexed.

"I don't want trouble. There was trouble in Tangier," growled the sailor and spat neatly against the side of the boat.

"It's a respectable house," retorted Charlie, who suspected that Mrs Reynolds' good name was in doubt.

The sailor laughed and made a final inspection of the cabbage patch before returning to his suitcase.

"Can you sell me a yam?"

"No rain," said Charlie. "Nothing fit to eat."

"I could murder a yam," sighed the sailor and returned to the road.

His name was Matthew Mark Luke Saint John and he entered Rams Horn at sunset. He walked slowly, the black boots bleached by dust and the suitcase perched on his broad shoulders. The streets were empty. A smell of seaweed and drains drifted up from Whelk Pier. The dying sun leaked a trail of blood and sizzled softly into the sea.

Two small boys followed the sailor through the town, whistling, hooting and running for their lives whenever he turned to threaten them with his fist. They followed him onto the esplanade and were thrilled to see him stand and spit at the sea. Mrs Clancy, pressed against her bedroom window, watched him walk down Regent Terrace and quickly wrapped herself in the curtains. She looked as if she had seen a ghost.

But Mrs Reynolds, sensing no danger, invited him into her house and boiled him a lobster.

Chapter Nine

"He was a darkie," said Smudger with relish.

"They walk around nude in tropical countries. I seen 'em on television," said Vernie.

"Why?" said Sickly.

"Because of the heat. It does something to 'em and they walk around in the stark staring nude," Vernie explained.

"Everybody?" said Smudger.

"Yes," said Vernie confidently. "That's why they're darkies."

"I wish I'd seen 'em on television," muttered Smudger miserably.

It was a blinding summer's day. Larks fluttered in a burning sky and the ditches were filled with nettles. The heat had drawn the perfume from the honeysuckle and, through the breaks in the hedgerows, the fields glittered with poppy and thistle. They had walked into the hills, high above Rams Horn and the smell of the Sheep, to seek shelter in their favourite camp.

"We could take off *our* clothes," suggested Sickly.

"It's not the same," said Smudger.

"It would be different," said Vernie, staring hard at Sickly, "if *she* was here."

Sickly had already explained the failure of his hypnotic power. He was small. He didn't have the strength to knock down fully-grown women and keep them sedated. It was obvious. Anyway, they should have known something was wrong when they had read *Your Secret Power to Command*. If it was so easy to hypnotise women why didn't everybody do it? If it was that easy, Sickly argued, most of the women in Rams Horn would be strolling the streets like sleep-walkers. He had done everything according to the instructions. He wasn't to blame that the plan had failed. Vernie and Smudger accepted his explanation but they couldn't hide their disappointment.

"We almost did it," Vernie reflected bitterly. "And then she woke up and spoiled everything."

They reached an old beech tree, glanced furtively around them and quickly went to earth among the roots where a family of badgers had excavated a tunnel in the soft chalk. The boys had turned the tunnel into a cave, the walls supported with chicken wire and the floor lined with fertilizer sacks but, even through the heat of high summer, it smelt of mildew and damp. They shivered as they huddled together in the gloom.

"I don't understand why it didn't work," said Smudger.

"It worked on Old George," Sickly reminded them. They had seen it for themselves.

"You said she wouldn't know anything about it. You said we could do anything," complained Smudger, watching a wood louse crawl over his shoes.

"Jesus, she nearly killed me," Vernie complained.

"She must have recognised us," said Smudger, shaking his head and wondering if he would be arrested.

"She was too frightened. She came out of the trance and she didn't know what was happening. That's why she ran out into the garden," said Sickly.

Vernie and Smudger were sceptical but they accepted his diagnosis. They had grave doubts about placing their faith again with Sickly but he was, after all, the only agent who could deliver his mother into their hot and inquisitive hands.

"What are we going to do now?" said Vernie. Above them, in the beech wood, a cuckoo stuttered as it chimed the hour.

"We could kidnap her and take her to the shed," said Smudger hopefully. He wanted Sickly's mother held captive in the shed so that he would have the opportunity to mount a secret, midnight rescue and win her gratitude. His reward involved various romantic adventures in which she begged him to sit guard and watch as she played in the bath or pleaded with him to sleep nude in her arms since she was frightened to be left alone.

"We already agreed the police would find her in the shed," said Sickly, and Smudger blushed and pretended to search for the wood louse inside his shoes.

"My old woman's got bad legs. The doctor gave her some sleeping pills," said Vernie, pulling the tobacco tin from his pocket and attempting to roll a cigarette with a little strip of newspaper.

"Do they work?" said Smudger.

"Yes. It's terrible. You can't wake her up again. She falls out of bed sometimes and just goes on sleeping," he said, sticking the cigarette into his mouth and searching for a box of matches. He struck a match and the cigarette fell apart.

"I've heard about 'em," said Smudger. "You swallow 'em and then you start to feel heavy and you can't keep your eyes open and so you just fall asleep."

Vernie nodded and pointed his finger at Sickly. "We want you to give her the sleeping pills. And then, when she's asleep we'll come and have a look," he said, spitting strands of tobacco through his teeth.

Sickly said nothing.

"She'll go to bed and when she's unconscious we can switch on the light," said Smudger, who was beginning to get the idea.

"And take off the bedclothes," said Vernie.

"And when we've finished we cover her up again. So she won't know anything about it," hooted Smudger. It was wonderful. Clean, efficient and irresistible. Science would conquer where magic had failed.

"They sound dangerous," said Sickly, doubtfully.

"No," said Vernie. "They come from the doctor. My old lady swears by them. They don't do you any harm. They just make you sleep."

Sickly was silent for a long time. He was sitting at the back of the cave where the pale roots curled around his head. A trickle of earth fell from the crumbling ceiling and he raised a hand to brush his ear. His face was dark but his eyes were shining.

"It's impossible," he said.

"Why?" hissed Vernie.

"Well, I can't just walk into her bedroom, grab her nose and push sleeping pills down her throat."

"You could pretend they were for headaches," said Smudger brightly.

"We can't wait for her to have a headache," Sickly protested. "It could take years."

"You crush 'em and mix 'em into the milk. The milk hides the taste," said Vernie, who had seen it on television.

"Does she drink milk?" asked Smudger.

"Yes, she has Bournvita before she goes to bed," said Sickly thoughtfully.

"It's perfect. She won't suspect nothing if she feels tired at night and she's going to bed. It's natural," said Vernie grinning.

"What time does she have her Bournvita?" said Smudger.

"About midnight."

"So it should be safe around two o'clock in the morning," said Vernie. "I can get out of my bedroom down the drain-pipe . . ."

"And I can climb through the kitchen window," said Smudger.

"But how will you steal the pills?" asked Sickly.

"I don't know. She keeps them locked away. But it shouldn't be difficult."

"She won't miss a few of 'em," said Smudger.

"Do you know what will happen if anything goes wrong?" said Vernie. He had stopped grinning and was staring mor-bidly at his plimsolls.

"No," said Sickly.

"We'll bury you alive," said Smudger.

"We'll bring you up here and break your arms and legs and

leave you to starve to death," said Vernie, slapping the walls of the cave with his hand.

Sickly glanced nervously around the earth dungeon and shivered. He thought of himself with his bones broken, alone in the darkness and the beech roots dripping through the rusty chicken wire.

"It will be days, weeks, before they find you," said Smudger.

"And it will be too late and they'll think it was an accident," said Vernie.

"That's right," said Smudger. "And we'll wait for the winter until we do it. We'll wait until you've almost forgotten and we'll catch you by surprise."

"One night, when it's cold and raining, we'll creep out of the darkness and murder you."

"You don't trust me," said Sickly, rubbing at his long, freckled nose.

"We trusted you last time."

"But I took all the risks," said Sickly indignantly.

"He did bring us her pants," said Smudger, whose thoughts had again returned to the shed.

"What else does she wear?" said Vernie.

"I don't know. It's difficult. She counts everything when she takes it out of the laundry basket," explained Sickly.

"Does she wear pyjamas?" inquired Vernie casually.

"No."

"Does she go to bed in the nude?" screeched Smudger, who seemed to think it was a scandal.

"No, she wears a sort of long nightdress, pink, with big sleeves," said Sickly.

"Can you see her legs or anything?"

"No, it goes down to the ground," he confessed.

"Oh," said Smudger, disappointed.

"But you can see through it," added Sickly.

"I don't believe him," sneered Vernie. His own mother wore pyjamas buttoned to the neck and gloves, too, in bad weather.

"It's true. You can see clean through it. That's why she wears a dressing-gown to cover it up when she's not actually in bed."

"But why does she wear it?" demanded Vernie. This new knowledge worried and perplexed him. It didn't make sense.

"I don't know," shrugged Sickly.

"I mean, if you can see through it and she covers it up so that you can't see through it, well, why does she wear it?" continued Vernie.

"Perhaps it makes her feel special," said Smudger, but he doubted it. He remembered wearing his mother's brassiere around the bathroom and it hadn't done anything for him.

"And how do you know you can see through it?" demanded Vernie suspiciously.

"Sometimes when she comes into my room and she thinks I'm asleep she doesn't bother with the dressing-gown and I can see everything," said Sickly smugly. He pulled a wrinkled ball of Bazooka from his pocket and pushed it into his mouth.

"Well, it doesn't make any difference," said Vernie. "If we give her the sleeping pills we can roll her around and take it off without any trouble."

"We can take it in turns to get into bed," said Smudger.

"And squeeze her snapper," wheezed Vernie.

"She won't wake up?" asked Sickly, blowing bubbles.

"No, you can't wake up my old lady. We tried all sorts. It's like she's dead but snoring."

"How many pills does she take at night?" asked Smudger, very impressed.

"Two."

"Is that enough?"

"Yes," said Vernie.

"I want four," said Sickly. "I don't want nothing to go wrong." He stretched the gum into a soft, pink bootlace and offered a length of it to Smudger.

"No thanks!" grunted Smudger in disgust.

"That's dangerous," warned Vernie.

"Why?" frowned Sickly, sucking the bootlace back into his mouth.

"You die if you swallow it," explained Smudger.

"That's stupid," snorted Sickly and blew another bubble.

"It's rubber and they discovered that when you swallow it,

the rubber melts and goes sticky and covers your pipes and everything," said Vernie.

"It's like drinking glue," explained Smudger enthusiastically. "Your stomach sticks together."

"And sometimes it blows itself into an enormous bubble so that you can't breathe no more and you die of suffocation," added Vernie.

"They wouldn't let you have the stuff if it was dangerous," said Sickly, chewing thoughtfully.

"They let you have sleeping pills – and they're dangerous," argued Vernie.

Sickly swallowed the gum and bared his teeth in a ghastly grin.

Chapter Ten

At dusk Tom Crow walks down from Rams Horn and sits on the rocks to wait for the moon. He had once been a lighthouse keeper. A wild old man who lived on a pillar far out in the wastes of the empty sea. The people who live in the town shiver when they see him at sunset. They think his years of loneliness must have driven him mad. But Tom Crow ignores them. At dusk he sits on the rocks until the moon floats over the sea and then he stands, knee-deep in shadow, and shouts and laughs as the moon lights the water.

The lighthouse held him for thirty years. When the motor launch brought him ashore he carried nothing but a bundle of clothes and a small metal box. Inside the box was a map of the heavens and a necklace made from fishbones.

No one wanted him. On that first night he walked from house to house asking for a room with a smell of the sea, but each time he was turned away and directed a little further down the road that led from the town. At last he arrived at a cottage built from the ribs of an old tramp steamer. It was raining and past midnight, the wind like a razor at his fingers. He banged on the door and shouted for food and shelter.

An enormous woman answered him. She was ugly and fat as a maggot. Her hair had been woven into a pigtail and she wore a blanket tied by a cord to her throat. She was so big that Tom Crow thought he'd disturbed a phantom.

Yet a thick, sweet perfume surrounded the woman, the

memory of fish soup, crab meat and peppers. The woman smiled. She led him into the warmth of the cottage and locked the door behind them.

There were candles burning and a great fire smouldered in the darkness. He stood in the centre of the room, his eyes raw with salt and his shoulders steaming. The woman asked no questions. She sat him down at the table and prepared him a bowl of pepper soup. He placed his parcel of clothes beneath his chair and held the battered tin box on his knees. Through the gloom of the smoking fire he could see long bundles of dried fish hanging from the ceiling beams. The timber walls held dark alcoves and hiding places for bags of potatoes, turnips and walnuts. A shabby carpet on the floor at his feet. Against one wall a mound of pillows and blankets.

When he had finished the soup Tom Crow sucked on his pipe and sat, comfortable in the silence, watching the woman move around in the twilight. It was an hour or more before he noticed the idiot girl squatting in a distant alcove, watching him.

She was fourteen years old and wore nothing but shoes. Her hair was as black as seaweed and her tiny breasts twinkled like starfish. Between her legs her pubis glowed as pink as the curl in a cowrie shell. This half-wit girl was the single fruit from a dozen nights spent with a Chinese sailor. She would not speak a sensible word but liked to sing in a language she shared with the seals. When Tom Crow returned her gaze the poor child whimpered and tried to hide her face in her hands, so that the mother had to pick her up and carry her off to the big, grey bed.

Safe among the pillows the idiot girl forgot the lighthouse keeper and began to sing her strange, thin song. The woman untied the blanket at her throat to cover the child and then, seeming to ignore the man, walked naked to the hearth. He watched as she bent to throw logs on the fire and the marrow began to melt in his bones. Her great buttocks rolled like the swell on a heavy, winter sea. There were fine black whiskers around her nipples so that, when he looked at her breasts as they hung in the smoke, he imagined huge catfish sniffing for scraps. He stared until his bones had turned as soft as eels and then he unlocked the box and took out the necklace. He called to the woman and stood on his chair to lock the trinket around her fat neck. She laughed as she felt the prickling spines. She gathered Tom Crow in her arms and gently placed him in bed beside the sleeping half-wit child.

For months no one saw him. And then, one dusk, he appeared on the rocks to shout at the moon. When they learned what had happened, the people in Rams Horn felt ashamed that he had been forced to share the house of this monstrous woman and the lunatic child. For a time they supposed he had died of neglect. The butcher offered him a room with a bible, a caged canary and a proper cooked breakfast. Mrs Reynolds tried to tempt him next with private plumbing and savoury dumplings. But Tom Crow would only grunt and shake his head.

They were puzzled by his refusal to join them. They could not understand it. The stubborn old fool. Why did he want to live among pagans when they could give him everything? How could he resist clean linen, fresh cabbage and a Christian burial? But Tom Crow smiles and says nothing.

Each evening, when the moon has lit the water, he goes home to the upturned tramp steamer and there, in the darkness of the blankets, he clambers aboard the enormous woman while her belly rolls like the vast Atlantic and the catfish jump and snap at his nose. He clings to the woman and catches the frightened idiot girl, pinching the little starfish breasts to make her struggle and sing her song. And when she sings he shuts his eyes and dreams he is dancing with mermaids.

Chapter Eleven

Long ago, before the lobstermen came to Rams Horn, when Britain was smothered in forest and bears lived in the mountains, Neolithic tribesmen settled on the hills above the Sheep. They grew crops, grazed cattle and stared at the stars in the clean, black sky. They were hypnotised by the movement of the heavens, afraid that the stars would fly down and eat them. For this reason they composed extravagant songs of praise to the sun at dawn. But the winters seemed eternal, the sun shrank and the stars blazed at noon. The little tribe was seized with melancholy. They burned their houses and slaughtered the cattle. On the sloping cliffs above the sea they built a stone burial chamber and covered it with a bank of earth. It was a long barrow of shingle and mud. A shield against the open sky. And, when it was finished, they crawled inside and died. The barrow concealed them and wild grass grew on its slippery shoulders.

When the Romans arrived the tomb had weathered into the rolling landscape. Before the hills had been claimed for Wessex, the daughters of Rams Horn were planting candles on the mound in a ceremony already so ancient that no one knew its origin. At Beltane in May virgins rolled down it. At Halloween fish-wives danced around it. Regency hypochondriacs slept on it. And the Victorians, hunting fossils, thought it a picturesque blister of earth and sketched it.

Sir Percy Wordsworth Wheel from the Isle of Wight was

the first man to identify and excavate the barrow. He had seen the Bronze Age barrows at Winterborne Poor Lot and examined the prehistoric fortifications at Maiden Castle. But Sir Percy was searching for the men of Atlantis. He believed that the Isle of Wight Needles were the ruined Pillars of Hercules, Atlantis had sunk in the English Channel and survivors washed up on the Dorset coast. It was his belief that these survivors had erected megalithic tombs in which to hide the wisdom of their race and the barrows at Rams Horn contained the secrets of eternity.

He began to probe the barrow on 8th June 1923. He worked slowly, cutting a trench towards the centre of the tomb. After several days of hard and unrewarding labour he felt discouraged but when Mount Etna erupted on the fifteenth of the month he knew he had disturbed the gods. He stopped work and considered the risks of looting the dead. There was a curse upon those who had raided the pyramids. Who knew what to expect from Atlantis? But the chance to have his own name written into the history books proved too much for him. On the afternoon of the last day of August he had reached the inner sanctum and waited overnight to remove the great stones. The next morning he heard that Tokyo and Yokohama had been destroyed by an earthquake with the loss of 100,000 lives. Sir Percy blamed himself. He filled the excavation with rubble and fled to his house on the Isle of Wight.

Now the barrow is a lost and forgotten shrine. A long, green teat on the breast of a hill that is sliding slowly into the sea. Snails cluster on the stones, skippers dance in the sunlight and, in the shelter of the tangled grass, bee orchids thrust out flowers disguised as the dark and hairy rumps of bumbles. But at night, when gulls walk the hills and the bats are flying like cinders, Tom Crow climbs the barrow to stare at the stars.

The doctor first met Tom Crow one evening in the saloon of the Dolphin. The long, gloomy parlour was empty. Wooden chairs were huddled in corners. A cat lay curled on one of the tables, wheezing softly in its sleep. There were framed photographs of shipwrecks on the walls, a lifebelt and a Guinness clock.

The doctor was drinking a bottle of cider and staring at a slice of Rams Horn sausage when Tom Crow came in from the street. He was a narrow ghost of a man with bad skin and hair like barbed wire. He wore a leather coat, boots and gauntlets; and carried a pair of motorcycle goggles to protect his eyes from the wind and the rain. He looked dressed to survive in hard and treacherous weather, as if he were planning to sleep in a hedge. He glared at the doctor and ordered a large brown rum. The doctor watched him. He had heard stories of Tom Crow.

The intruder carried his drink carefully to a distant table. A canvas satchel hung from his shoulders and he had to struggle to unharness himself before he could sit in the chair. When he was free he sucked at the rum and sighed. The clock creaked. The cat sneezed. The doctor returned to his cider. And then a voice, calling through the glass screen that divided saloon from snug, broke the silence.

"Are you going out on the hills again, Tom?" called the voice with a snigger.

"Yes," barked Tom without glancing up from his rum.

"It's a fine night for it," cackled the voice and there was a muffled roar of laughter from the snug.

"Are you looking for something?" asked the doctor as he smiled at Tom.

"That's right."

"Flying machines," boomed the landlord. "He's looking for flying machines from another planet." He banged his fist on the bar, wiped the hand and sniffed his fingers.

The doctor stopped smiling and quickly finished his cider. "Do you see many?" he asked as he cradled the empty glass in his hand.

"I don't expect you to believe it," growled Tom. "But when they arrive they'll find me waiting." He gave the doctor a long, penetrating stare and slapped his gauntlets against the edge of the table.

"Martians are the only people who want to listen to him, the daft bugger," growled Big Lily White.

The doctor, embarrassed, picked up a knife and looked at

64

his plate of sausage. But the light, filtered through a red paper lampshade, gave the sausage a poisonous glow.

"How long have you been waiting, Tom?" laughed the voice from the snug.

"We've been waiting for thousands of years," replied Tom, still staring at the doctor. "They wrote about them in the Bible. They built the pyramids as beacons for them."

"Why haven't they come before?" shouted Big Lily White.

"They've been waiting until we need them."

"Who?"

"Them," grunted Tom impatiently. "The voyagers from beyond the stars. They've been waiting, out there, on the edge of the galaxy."

"Have you ever seen them?" asked the doctor.

Tom Crow sniffed and grinned. He picked up his glass and drained it. "I've seen things you wouldn't believe."

"Do you always watch from the barrow?"

"That's right. The hill has been charged with energy. When there's a storm you can feel it vibrating under your feet. I think it's a beacon. When they arrive they'll use it to guide them."

"What makes you think they're out there?"

Tom frowned. "There has to be something out there," he said.

"Why?"

"He thinks they're going to save the world," jeered Big Lily White.

"He thinks they're going to buy him another rum," called the voice from the snug.

"It's written in the Bible," said Tom with a shrug.

The doctor was silent. You couldn't argue with old Tom Crow. He held strong views about the world. He had studied history and he knew there was nothing on earth that could save man from himself. And so he had turned to the heavens.

"I'd like to come out one night," said the doctor, after his second bottle of cider. He was impressed by the simple, stubborn faith of the man. He wanted to know what he saw when he stood on the hills with his hair stiff with frost and his eyes full of moonlight.

"There's nothing for you out there."

"I'm a doctor."

"I never use one. I don't believe in it."

"But they might need one when they arrive," said the doctor. It was a crafty argument and poor Tom was mad enough to believe it.

"How's that?" he said.

"They might suffocate in oxygen," said the doctor quietly.

"Or they might injure themselves – the cliffs are dangerous at night," said Tom, squinting at the shipwrecks on the wall.

"A doctor might save them."

"But we don't know when they'll arrive."

"That's not important. Take me out with you one night. And then, whenever they arrive, you can call on me for help."

"You'll be going out at your own risk," growled Tom. "I can't be responsible for you."

The following evening the doctor met Tom in the Dolphin and, at closing time, fortified with a flask of rum, they walked out along the cliff path to the barrow. The doctor was wrapped against the cold and armed with a heavy, rubber torch. Tom Crow marched ahead of him, impatient and excited, the satchel slapping against his shoulders. They followed the path up through the crumbling hills until Rams Horn was reduced to a phosphorescent puddle that flickered beneath their feet. When they reached the barrow a slice of moon gave enough light to help them climb the treacherous bank. They squatted, breathless, in the long grass and stared at the sky. The stars burned gently around their ears.

"This hill was built thousands of years ago by men who came from across the sea. They didn't have machines to move the earth. They used the power of their imaginations. That's another secret we've lost," whispered Tom as he wrestled with the satchel. He unbuckled the bag and produced a small, brass telescope.

"But think of all the secrets we've discovered," argued the

doctor. "Look at all the advances we've made in medicine." He wanted to sing in praise of miracles manufactured in the laboratory, the skills of the specialist, the precision of the surgeon's knife but, since modern medicine in Rams Horn meant a bottle of Mrs Halibut's elixir of life, he no longer had the faith to celebrate. "We live longer than our grandfathers," he added doubtfully.

"Why?"

The doctor was silent. It was a question he had been trained to ignore. He had been sent into the world to stitch, glue, plug and bandage. Life was machinery that needed proper maintenance, fuel and spare parts.

"We must cling to life," he said quietly.

"Nonsense," snapped Tom. "God created the universe by simple arithmetic. The multiplication of dust. You can't kill dust."

"But we must have made some progress," insisted the doctor, trying to imagine what men had achieved since they had left the swamp.

"Boots, bayonets, bullets and bombs," said Tom. A cruel wind whipped at the grass and he pulled down his goggles. He looked like a marooned aviator and the doctor wondered if he might not be searching for his own, lost flying machine among the distant stars.

"What do you think they'll do when they arrive, Tom?"

"They'll explain everything. It has to mean something, doesn't it? They'll explain it." His eyes were anxious. His breath was a rushing cloud of steam.

Yes, thought the doctor, they'll explain everything. Nothing is impossible. And he thought of himself sitting in Storks Yard, the door locked, the fire blazing and Mrs Clancy held naked under his healing hands. "Perhaps they'll come tomorrow," he said. He peered up into the sky, half-expecting to see shadows against the stars, strange lights on the wind, faces staring down from heaven. He uncorked the flask and filled his mouth with rum.

"I've been waiting a long time," said Tom, glancing at his luminous wristwatch. "Perhaps it's too late." And he looked so sad that the doctor wanted to wrap his arms around him for comfort.

"Do you think there'll be a war?"

Tom shrugged. "It makes no difference. We poison everything we touch. We don't need a war to destroy ourselves. That's progress. I'm old. I'm glad. I won't be here to see the end."

They never saw the flying machines and perhaps, after all, the barrow was no more than a common grave full of farmers' bones. But it was enough for the doctor to be standing on that great, black hump of earth, drinking rum with Tom Crow and watching the stars, while the sea whispered, soft as the rustle of women's skirts, below in the darkness.

Chapter Twelve

"Beyond Weymouth is the ancient town of Rams Horn, whose inhabitants catch lobster, mackerel and other fish. There is little to recommend Rams Horn to the traveller. But here you may find an uncommonly fine sausage. The local people use pork scraps for the purpose, seasoned with pepper, walnuts, onions, sage, and thickened with blood. The sausages have a dark, distinctly speckled appearance and a very strong flavour, similar to the venison sausages of the New Forest. They are sold in long links and traditionally eaten cold with potato pie. When pork is unavailable the poor wives of Rams Horn use chicken, rabbit or rook meat, softened in cider. These sausages are generally boiled and served with eggs and cabbage. But a number of the older women continue to hang them in smoke, leaving them often until they are rotten and fall from the chimneys in strings. They have a queer smell and a wrinkled appearance, although many in the town have a taste for them and like to eat them with bread and a glass of young beer."

A Rustic Guide to England and Wales, 1924

Chapter Thirteen

Matthew Mark Luke Saint John felt at home in Rams Horn. He liked the smell of the big, grey sea as it rolled against the esplanade and the stewed smell of bladderwrack and mussels when the water drained from the piles of the pier. He liked the way the sunlight smoked through the net curtains of his little bedroom, the colour of the rosebud wallpaper and the sight of his suitcase tucked securely under the bed. He liked the silence of the house.

For the first few days he rarely left his room, appearing only briefly at breakfast and supper to smile shyly at Mrs Reynolds and demolish a lobster, a rabbit or pineapple pie. But Mrs Reynolds encouraged him to sit with her after his meals, read the newspapers and talk of his adventures.

She liked to have a man in the house: the tread of boots on the stairs and the smell of shaving soap in the bathroom basin. There was something about the size and shape of the man that made her feel deliciously dainty. When Matthew Mark Luke Saint John sat on her sofa he looked so clumsy among the tiny, embroidered cushions and lace antimacassars that she felt a mere ornament beside him.

She noticed, with surprise, that the effect on Polly was less exhilarating. Her daughter, who was usually so wild, seemed intimidated by the big, black sailor. She ate with them in silence, hardly daring to glance from her plate and at the slightest excuse tried to lock herself away in her room.

70

"Sit down," Mrs Reynolds would shout when the truculent child tried to slip away and pouting Polly would rush from the house, her face flushed and her eyes shining with tears.

"You must excuse Polly. She can be difficult sometimes," apologised Mrs Reynolds as she offered her guest a plate of biscuits.

"She's young," said the sailor as he snapped a biscuit with his thumb.

"She's sixteen," said Mrs Reynolds.

"A child."

"I wish I could believe it," sighed Mrs Reynolds. The girl was a mystery. Her breasts had sprouted beneath her vest and yet she refused to give up the secret society of children. She wore socks with her skirts and slept with a one-eyed bear.

"It must be hard without a man," said the sailor sympathetically.

"You never married?" she inquired.

Matthew Mark Luke Saint John shook his head. "The sea is a cruel woman," he said. He tossed the broken biscuit into his mouth and crunched it sadly.

"Yes, I can imagine," said Mrs Reynolds. The sea is a cruel woman. It sounded like wisdom from a Christmas cracker.

"She'll rock you to sleep in her arms and drown you while you're dreaming. If she doesn't break your heart she'll break your bones."

"You must miss your home, sometimes, when you're out there on the water."

The sailor closed his eyes and sighed.

"We were a simple people. We ate the fruit of the forest and feasted on the fish of the sea. The spirits of the dead lived inside a great volcano and if we were wicked they filled the sky with smoke," he said. He invented everything. He had been born in Victoria, an English seaside town on the coast of Cameroon in West Africa. The town was surrounded by a monotony of rubber and palm plantations. The volcano was a cold, grey cone perpetually wrapped in rain. His mother had been a Crusader for Jesus. His father sold Toyota spare parts. As a child Matthew Mark Luke Saint John had dreamt of the city and, at the first opportunity, he ran away to live in Douala. He fried hamburgers all day and slept, at night, with a girl from the dance hall. He worked hard to make his fortune. But the restaurant burned down and the girl ran away with a French shoe salesman. The big city had disappointed him. He moved south through Gabon and into the Congo where he found work on the short-sea traders that sail from Pointe-Noire.

It wasn't much of a story and he knew Mrs Reynolds expected tales of a lost jungle paradise. She saw Africa as a prehistoric forest of steaming undergrowth crawling with panthers, pygmies and spiders. There were no cities, no highways and no hamburgers in her Africa. And so he contrived to speak of the world she saw in her imagination.

Sometimes he claimed Bantu ancestors and, at other times, he boasted he could trace his family back five hundred years to the royal family of the Kongo kingdom. The pleasure in Mrs Reynolds' eyes encouraged him to concoct a fantasy of alarming proportions. He spoke of the snakes that swallowed babies, the giant apes that kidnapped women and, although he had never seen an elephant, he described how a rogue bull had entered the village one night and killed his grandmother.

When he grew tired of this game he talked of his years at sea. Mrs Reynolds asked questions and he was happy to answer them, flattered by her curiosity. He had been to the Caribbean and the Gulf of Mexico. He had sailed the Indian Ocean as far as the Bay of Bengal. Why he had come to Rams Horn, however, remained a mystery. He claimed to want nothing more than solitude and rest from his travels. Mrs Reynolds preferred to think of him as a fugitive from some ghastly crime, the mysterious and violent stranger that Mrs Clancy had seen in the crystal. She loved to sit and make the sailor talk.

But one afternoon, when lunch was finished, Matthew Mark Luke Saint John could not be persuaded to sit and provide her entertainment. He scratched and yawned and complained of the heat. She tried to keep him talking but at last he excused himself and went to his room. Mrs Reynolds sat alone. Polly had cycled to Drizzle. The house was silent. She tried to read but could not concentrate. Sunlight flared against the windows, the room smelt of carpets, the air was heavy with the boredom of heat. She picked up her sewing but quickly abandoned it – the fine stitching hurt her eyes. She thought she might visit poor Mrs Clancy but, once she had found her sandals, could not find the energy to confront the scorching, narrow streets. She felt restless and uncomfortable.

Finally she ran a bath, lowered the blinds and let herself float in the cool water. Were there really giant apes who kidnapped women? Her skin looked very white in the twilight. She stared at her legs, her belly and breasts. She looked so pale she fancied she would shine in the dark. She thought of Matthew Mark Luke Saint John alone in his room. She imagined him asleep in the little bed, the curtains drawn, his body black as a shadow against the sheets. What wild and tropical shore did he reach in his dreams? Did he visit tattooed women with oiled hair and skin the colour of ink? And what if he should suddenly wake, anxious to pass water, stupid with sleep, forgetting his surroundings and stumble naked to the bathroom? The door was unlocked and they were alone in the house. If she lay very quiet, would he notice her there in the bath? She thought of him standing, head bent, legs braced against the porcelain bowl. And she smiled as she rolled the soap between her hands.

She dried herself carefully, brushed the copper curls away from her ears and then, dressed in a fresh cotton wrapper, went barefoot to the kitchen to make lemonade. He would need lemonade if he'd fallen asleep in the afternoon heat. It was no trouble. She would not disturb him. She could slip into his room, leave the jug and be gone before he woke. It was nothing. And, anyway, he probably slept in his shirt.

She poured the lemonade and crept upstairs. When she reached the sailor's bedroom she opened the door slowly, without a sound, afraid she might wake him before she had reached the bed.

Matthew Mark Luke Saint John was sitting on the floor reading a bible. He glanced up and smiled at Mrs Reynolds as she came, dancing on tiptoe, into the room.

"I've brought you a cold drink," she whispered. She felt

rather foolish, as if she had been caught trying to steal something from him.

"Thank you," he said. He was wearing a pale blue shirt and a pair of threadbare trousers. The sleeves of the shirt were rolled to his elbows.

She sat carefully down on the edge of the bed and looked around the room. Everything was clean, polished and just as she had arranged it for him. There was a cheap alarm clock on the bedside cabinet. The wardrobe had been locked. The bookshelf was empty. He had disturbed nothing.

"Do you read the good book?" he said, smiling and closing the bible with a slap.

Mrs Reynolds shook her head. She had never taken to the church. She found the whole business of saints and sinners rather tedious and suspected that God might have invented the idea of sin for the pleasure of being the only power in Heaven or Hell with the authority to wash it away. The local faithful, most of whom had never been near a good, red-blooded sin in their lives, seemed to find a thrill in being found guilty of unholy crimes and attending the church at Drizzle for a weekly wash and brush-up. Oh yes, it was obviously very good for the soul but no matter how patiently she tried to marinate her own soul in the acid of guilt, it never quite worked. They must have taken out her guilt along with her tonsils when she was a girl. If they had left it alone it might have grown to be a great, wobbly cyst burning away beneath her ribs. Something to make a woman proud to be a sinner. Something to flaunt at the priest. How could you be a good Christian without it?

But that wasn't the reason she had abandoned the church. She had stopped attending services because of the singing. It might have been different if the flock was expected to dance. She enjoyed dancing. But the prospect of spending Sundays droning through a torn copy of *Ancient and Modern* with a hundred wheezing old ladies smelling of moth balls and eucalyptus was enough to make her surrender her ticket to Heaven. She didn't regret it for a moment. It was rumoured they even sang in Heaven.

"I thought you might have a different god," she said, dreaming of little yellow idols with ivory fangs and amethyst eyes.

Matthew Mark Luke Saint John sat on the floor and laughed. It was a huge shout of laughter that made him throw back his head and bare his teeth like a yawning tiger. Mrs Reynolds blushed.

"There are gods and devils enough for everyone," he said, wiping his eyes with the palm of his hand. His mother had been a Crusader for Jesus but as a boy he had met men from the North who could cast spells, tread hot coals and swallow live scorpions.

"Yes," said Mrs Reynolds. "I'm sorry."

"My mother gave me this bible."

"It's beautiful."

"Crocodile skin."

"Lovely."

"You don't hold the faith?"

"No," said Mrs Reynolds. "But my husband enjoyed the odd sermon, God rest him."

"Your husband?"

"A tragedy."

"Yes?"

"He fell off the roof and damaged his brains."

"When did this happen?" he said.

"Oh, years ago. Polly was a baby. But I'll never forget it. He hit the pavement with such a bang that I thought he was dead."

"He survived?" inquired the sailor. As he spoke he picked up her foot and held it lightly in his hand. The touch was warm, dry, innocent. He smiled and gazed at the foot as if he were admiring an expensive shoe.

"He came to the kitchen, sat down and ate a tongue sandwich."

"A miracle," he said. He ran his thumb along her toes. She trembled but she did not resist. Her foot glowed in his smooth, dark hand.

"There wasn't a scratch on him. He went to bed and I

thought, well, he'd had a lucky escape. You read about these things sometimes."

"And then?" whispered the sailor. His hand embraced the heel of her foot, his fingers coiling on the ankle.

"He woke up in the morning and he was a vegetable."

"No!" breathed the sailor. His hand held her calf, the fingers caressing the heavy, white curve.

"Yes," whispered Mrs Reynolds. "He just sat there and stared at me. I used to sit him in Polly's pram and push him around the house. It was horrible with his arms and legs dangling out and everything. I had to feed him with a spoon." She was breathless with fright, tantalized by the surreptitious journey of the sailor's fingers.

"What happened to him?"

"We had to put him away."

"You're not to blame yourself," said Matthew Mark Luke Saint John. His fingers tightened their grip, making her gasp. He pulled at her leg until the cotton wrapper fell away from her belly and thighs, his eyes feverish with desire. She blushed beneath the gluttony of his stare and tried to shield herself with her hands.

"They don't know what it's like to live with a vegetable," she croaked.

"It's no company," he said. He jerked her legs open so that she fell back upon the bed, suffocated with excitement and terror. She struggled to rise again, squirming and kicking with her feet, but he caught her by the ankles and held her down.

Mrs Reynolds closed her grey eyes and surrendered herself to the sailor's curiosity. She sensed him hesitate for a moment, felt the heat of his breath against her skin, and then he forced his face between her thighs and attacked her with a loose and greedy mouth, like a man sucking at a torn fruit. She cried out. She screamed. But when he pulled back his head in alarm she clawed at his scalp and forced his head down again, holding him prisoner with her knees. She lay back among the pillows, battered, bruised, and triumphant.

It was late when Polly came home. Matthew Mark Luke

Saint John was soaking in a cool bath. Mrs Reynolds was sitting in the safety of her bed, sipping at a jug of warm lemonade.

Chapter Fourteen

The sea sucked at the crumbling cliffs. The moon smouldered. Poisonous cats with yellow eyes crawled from the safety of drains and Rams Horn creaked in the darkness. At midnight, Tanner Atkins sat with the butcher in the parlour of the Dolphin and shared a dozen bottles of Badger with the weary landlord.

"Monica Monkhouse takes a tumble with Bernie the playful paratrooper," cackled Tanner. He was reading a copy of *Skirt*. His face shone with delight.

"You'll go blind reading this rubbish," snorted the landlord, snatching at the magazine and scornfully thumbing the pages.

"Is that right?" said Tanner.

"It overheats the blood," said Oswald Murdoch. "Women won't be safe in their beds tonight."

"I've never been very good with women," grieved Tanner.

"You're too old to worry about it," said Oswald.

"I have dreams sometimes," confessed Tanner. "Nothing nasty. I have dreams I'm sitting with some woman and she's wearing a white dress and white gloves and eating a box of Black Magic."

"What happens?" asked Big Lily White.

"She always chooses the soft centres," said Tanner, shaking his head.

"And then what happens?" demanded Oswald Murdoch.

"I don't know. It gets me so excited I wake up. I'm not very good with women. I talk to them but you can see they're not interested. They stare clean through me. I'm not deformed or anything like that. I mean, I look all right. I'm just not very good with them."

"You've got to know how to handle them – that's the secret," said Big Lily White.

"Is that right?" said Tanner.

"Give me two hours with a woman – any woman – and I can teach her to faint at the sight of me," boasted Big Lily White. "Women will give you anything if you know how to handle them."

"It's easy for someone like you," argued Oswald.

The landlord shrugged. "You need practice, of course, it's like anything else." A moth whirled through one of the windows and fluttered blindly against the wall.

"It's different when you're married," moaned Oswald Murdoch, wagging his head.

Big Lily White thought of the butcher in bed on a Sunday, surrounded by newspapers, toast crumbs and sunlight, with the comforting warmth of his wife beside him. "I hate sleeping with the same woman twice," he said defiantly. "It's funny but once I've done 'em I don't like 'em."

"I don't know," said Tanner. "A man needs a wife."

"A wife isn't a woman," said Big Lily White. He tried to imagine the violation of Oswald Murdoch's wife, tied to a chair by her apron strings, shouting with pain and screaming with pleasure, Lily you've made me feel like a woman, a frying pan full of eggs on the floor.

"I'm not complaining," said Oswald Murdoch. He picked up his glass, drained it and poked among the empty bottles on the table.

"I don't regret anything," said Big Lily White, dreaming of buttocks behind a clean apron, the smell of soap flakes, fruit cakes and floor wax, making love in his carpet slippers, wet afternoons in a friendly kitchen.

For some minutes they were silent, staring mournfully down at their glasses, stunned by the sadness of the world.

"There are times when I wonder – you know – if things had been different," whispered Oswald Murdoch.

"I've seen women do things that would poison your liver," muttered Big Lily White.

"What sort of things?" said Oswald Murdoch.

But Big Lily White was far away in a warm cottage, a woman to call his wife beside him, the smell of cut flowers in a china bowl, the cat asleep beneath the bed.

"What sort of things?" insisted Oswald.

"Women!" roared Big Lily White. "Fat women, nude women, wrestling in mud, kicking like shire horses. Thin women, rubber women, tied in knots with their tongues hanging out."

"Women," sobbed Oswald Murdoch, banging the table and knocking the bottles to the floor.

"Women!" wailed Big Lily White.

"I don't understand," bleated Tanner Atkins, his sleeves slopping in a puddle of beer. "I don't understand."

Big Lily White stood up and, leaning forward, clasped Oswald's head in his great, gnarled hands. "I love you," he managed to mumble. He closed his eyes, smiled, slid under the table and fell asleep.

Tanner sniffed and wiped his nose. His face was white. His hair was hanging in strings. "Sometimes you need to talk to a man," he sobbed.

"That's right," said Oswald.

And they cradled each other for comfort as they staggered from the Dolphin into the empty town.

Chapter Fifteen

The sailor was late for breakfast the next morning. Mrs Reynolds scratched at a slice of toast with her knife and tried to conceal her excitement. She felt intoxicated by the sound of the toast, the smell of coffee, the touch of sunlight on the white linen tablecloth, the colour of the marmalade as it glowed in the bowl. Her skin burned and her breasts felt swollen. It seemed to Mrs Reynolds that her daughter could not fail to notice the transformation. But Polly sat sulking and appeared to sense nothing.

Mrs Reynolds was relieved. She knew she couldn't protect the child forever and she didn't want them separated by secrets. But she would certainly prefer her daughter to grow into a woman without the memory of her mother's legs thrown around the shoulders of a giant African sailor.

The thought that Polly might have discovered them together made her drop the marmalade spoon. How could she have taken the risk? It was shocking. She had been overwhelmed by the full, primitive force of the man. She had not encouraged or teased him. It had been one of those abrupt and hungry encounters that happen without warning and, under the circumstances it was best to forgive and forget. The poor man had been hot and confused. It would never happen again. She heard footsteps on the stairs and composed her face in a look of absolute innocence. When Matthew Mark Luke Saint John appeared she stared at him as if he were a stranger and, when he sat down, ignored him. It was Polly, blushing, who had to pour him coffee.

He was polite, smiling and hungry for toast and Rams Horn sausage, which he ate in slices spread with lime pickle. He did not gloat at Mrs Reynolds but stared at his plate and tried talking to Polly.

"Are you going to school, today?" he said, spooning sugar into the coffee.

"Holidays," said Polly. Every day he asked the same question and received the same answer but it never failed to amuse him. She hated it.

"What will you do with yourself?" he chuckled.

Polly shrugged, glanced towards the door and Mrs Reynolds knew she was already thinking of escape.

"When I came down the road into the town I met a man who lives on a boat in a cabbage patch," said Matthew Mark Luke Saint John.

"That's Mr Bloater."

"Bloater," said the sailor thoughtfully. He glanced at Polly, opened his mouth and sucked down a slice of sausage.

"He smells of cabbages," she whispered and wrinkled her nose in disgust.

Matthew Mark Luke Saint John grinned. He hooked a shred of meat from his teeth with a fingernail. "I want you to go out there and give him something," he said.

"What is it?" said Polly.

The sailor was wearing a shapeless blue jacket and from the pocket he pulled a beer bottle which he carefully placed on the table.

"A gift," he announced.

Polly pulled the tangle of hair from her face and stared at the bottle. There, through the green and cloudy glass, she saw a boat sailing in a crinkled sea. It was a strange, carved boat with many masts and tiny strips of rag for sails. She pursed her lips and frowned.

"It's made from bones," said Matthew Mark Luke Saint John.

"Horrible," said Mrs Reynolds, leaning forward to peer at the curious skeleton.

"I bought it from a trader in Grand Bassam and he bought it from a tribesman in Guinea. They say they're human bones," he added, looking at her for the first time.

"Is Mr Bloater a friend?" she enquired.

"He directed me to this house," said Matthew Mark Luke Saint John, as if that explained everything and Mrs Reynolds began to blush as bright as Polly.

"Will you take my gift to Mr Bloater?"

"Yes," said Polly.

Mrs Reynolds watched in surprise as her daughter took the bottle from the sailor's hands. It was remarkable. She seemed suddenly to have lost her fear of the man. Or was it only the opportunity to own a bottle of bones for the morning that had lent her the courage? Well, it made no difference. She was glad that Polly had stayed with them for breakfast. It had helped to cover her own embarrassment.

She wrapped the bottle into the little saddlebag on Polly's bicycle and stood at the door to watch her daughter pedal away down the esplanade. She looked so small and vulnerable, perched on the clumsy machine as it flew into the sunlight, that Mrs Reynolds felt her heart squeezed with love for the child.

When she went back to the breakfast room Matthew Mark Luke Saint John was sitting in an armchair, reading the newspaper and sucking his teeth. He paid no attention as she cleaned the table and, reluctantly, Mrs Reynolds retired to the kitchen.

The passion of the previous afternoon already seemed a remote and capricious madness. She took a basket of raspberries from the pantry and began to clean them. They perfumed the water and stained her hands as she rolled them around the bucket in search of maggots. Did he feel ashamed of his brief and rapturous assault upon her person? He had betrayed nothing at breakfast. The desire had flared and died in him, leaving nothing but silence and regret. She spread a cloth on the kitchen table and piled the raspberries in a purple pyramid. How she loved those dark and hairy nipples of fruit. As she walked back and forth she snatched at them, one by one, pushed them into her mouth and exploded them between her teeth. Polly would be gone for hours. She would exhibit the bottle of bones to her friends before she made the delivery on the Upton Gabriel Road. She was such a strange child. Mrs Reynolds plucked at another raspberry but it jumped from her hand and rolled across the floor. She stooped to retrieve the fruit when something warm brushed her leg and she screamed.

She struggled to straighten herself but, as she turned, her skirt flew over her head and buried her in darkness. She spluttered and cried for help. But a huge hand clasped her head, forcing it down against her chest, while clumsy fingers pulled at her thighs.

"No," she screeched as she felt her underwear torn to shreds.

"Yes," he growled as he lifted her from her shoes and carried her to the kitchen table.

"No," she gasped as she folded against the edge of the table. Her arms were thrown across the wet fruit and her buttocks raised towards her assailant.

"Yes," he roared as he fought with the buckle of his belt.

"No," she moaned, bursting raspberries in her fists.

"Yes," he grunted. And with her head still wrapped in her skirt and her buttocks spread in his mighty hands she was hardly in a position to argue with him.

When it was finished she capsized and fell to the floor in a puddle of bleeding raspberries. She was so shaken that she took to her bed. But he continued to prowl the house, huge, naked and defiant.

He could not satisfy his hunger. He attacked her in the bathroom, the pantry and the linen cupboard. He pulled her down when she passed his chair and used his teeth to crack off the buttons on her skirt. He made her crawl across the floor on her hands and knees with her breasts hanging loose from her dress. For two weeks she was kept a prisoner in her own house. He followed her from room to room, broke in upon her when she washed, pulled at her clothes when she dressed and crept to her bed while she slept.

"Leave me alone," she pleaded, waking at dawn in a tangle of sheets to find him sucking at her breasts.

"You called me in your sleep," he growled, and she believed him.

She was consumed by the madness of the man. She was afraid sometimes that he'd stolen her soul and dragged her into slavery. She felt safe from him only when Polly was there and the sailor was forced to sit impatiently in his room, smouldering and silent. But these were brief interludes since Mrs Reynolds found excuses to keep Polly running errands while she, herself, contrived to stay at home. She thought she might remain the concubine of this wild and naked pagan giant for the rest of her life and noticed, with pride, that the shoes in her wardrobe were already gathering dust.

But there came a morning when hunger forced her into the streets in search of bacon, bread and fresh fruit.

"I could murder a yam," he said wistfully, as he watched her prepare to leave the house.

"I could look for a pineapple," she suggested.

"No. Bring me a lobster and a basin of shrimps," he said. He pulled a leather purse from his pocket and dropped it neatly into her hand.

"Thank you," she said. The purse felt so heavy she was sure it contained ducatoons.

"Will it take long?" he asked as she turned to leave. His great hands fluttered across her breasts, hesitated at her waist and disappeared in the folds of her skirt. His fingers rummaged anxiously for the naked heat of her legs.

"I haven't been out for weeks," she laughed, pulling away from his embrace and running into the street.

Chapter Sixteen

It was already late. The raw heat of the sun had softened the tar between the flagstones on the esplanade and the town stood, shuttered and exhausted, above a bleached and bubbling sea. She climbed up the cobbled hill to the high street, excited by the noise of the traffic and glad to be free from the house. She searched for yams among the sacks of carrots and potatoes in the empty supermarket. She looked at the fancy underwear in Modern Fashions. She passed the time of day with Horace, the fishmonger, and asked the health of his mother. On the corner of Anchor Road she paused to flirt with Oswald Murdoch through the curtain of hollow pigs he had strung across his counter.

"I've got something for you," he grinned as he beckoned her into the blood-stained darkness.

"And what is it?" she asked innocently.

"A nice, big tongue," he said and wiped his hands on his purple apron.

"No, I don't fancy it," she replied, wrinkling her nose.

"They're fresh," drooled Oswald Murdoch. "They're still steaming." He picked one up and flopped it over his arm.

"Do you have any chicken livers?"

"No," he said. "But the pork is good and plump. Come here and I'll let you squeeze it."

Mrs Reynolds tossed her head and skipped back into the

sunlight. She went up the hill as far as the Post Office and picked through the books and magazines.

But after an hour of walking she felt trapped by the little town. She was hot and tired. The Sheep stank, the paint was peeling from Whelk Pier and even the elegant sweep of Regent Terrace, with its fluted columns and dainty iron balconies, seemed tawdry and absurd. She had planned to visit Mrs Clancy, take a brandy and inquire about the next magic circle, but she felt impatient to be home again with the sailor. There, in the comfort of her parlour, she had learned to cast her own magic. When she snapped her fingers parrots flew into the air. When she raised her arms flamingoes danced on the carpet. When she opened her legs baboons screamed, panthers slunk forward on velvet bellies, drums began to vibrate across the length of Africa. She felt sad for her old friend, living her days without a man, spending her nights with the ghost of a husband.

Mrs Reynolds turned towards the esplanade and, with a lobster under her arm and a basket full of shrimps, hurried back to the house where Mrs Clancy's demon king was held, a fierce and hungry captive.

When she unlocked the front door she noticed Polly's bicycle leaning against the wall. She frowned as she unloaded her shopping in the kitchen. Polly had gone to Drizzle. What had happened to bring the child home so early in the afternoon? She walked into the parlour. Polly's sandals were thrown beneath a chair. Beside the chair a plate of broken biscuits. Crumbs on the carpet at her feet. She stood among the crumbs and held her breath, listening for the sounds of life. The house felt abandoned. And then, through the ceiling, she heard a muffled groan. It was a queer, suffocated noise that stiffened the hair on her neck. Her legs buckled. Her skin went cold.

She turned and ran towards her daughter's bedroom, her skirt ballooning, her legs leaping at the stairs. But when she burst through the door she stood, paralysed with horror, unable to understand what she saw among the broken dolls and nursery furniture. Her mouth sagged open, a crimson wound.

Polly was sprawled naked on the bed, her arms and legs pinned beneath the weight of the massive, half-dressed sailor. She rolled her head from side to side on the mangled pillows, gnashing her teeth and forcing out the most terrible moans. The sound of her distress seemed to excite the sailor to greater extremes of violence, so that he took hold of her wrists and held them above her head, pressing himself against her belly, spreading his mouth against her teeth and sucking the breath from her body. She kicked out feebly with her legs and the groans were stifled in her throat.

The sailor wore nothing but a vest and with every thrust of his body he gave a dark and threatening growl.

"Do you love me?" gasped Polly as they struggled.

"I love you," growled the sailor and pushed her wrists deeper into the pillows.

"Will you always love me?" she moaned.

"I'll always love you," muttered her assailant and sucked at her throat.

"Forever?" whispered the child hopefully. "Will you love me forever?"

"Forever," he promised and stopped her mouth with his tongue.

Mrs Reynolds stormed across the room, grabbed a hairbrush from the dressing-table and held it like a dagger in her fist. She leapt upon the sailor's back, held him fast with her knees and plunged the dagger between his shoulder-blades. He screamed in furious surprise and she stabbed him again, cracking the handle of the brush. He gurgled. He groaned. He tried to throw her off but she continued to ride him, twisted his head and dragged him to the floor.

"For God's sake, what's happening?" screeched the wounded sailor as he rolled over the carpet and clawed at his punctures.

Polly sprang into a crouch and stared with terrified eyes at the sight of her mother.

"Help," she squeaked. "He tried to attack me."

But Mrs Reynolds ignored the girl. She scrambled towards the sailor, grabbed a foot in her hands and sank her teeth into

88

the damp and naked flesh. He kicked out and somersaulted against the wall, howling and gathering his feet against his stomach.

"I'm bleeding to death," he roared, as he staggered to his feet.

"What have you done?" shrieked Mrs Reynolds, pointing towards the bed.

"You've torn me to ribbons," bawled the sailor. He made a rush for the dressing table and tried to inspect the damage in the mirrors.

"I'll kill you," screamed Mrs Reynolds.

"I tried to stop him," sobbed Polly. She shook her head and burst into tears.

Mrs Reynolds, fighting for breath, picked up the hair brush and hurled it at the frightened philanderer. The brush cracked one of the mirrors and caught the sailor a nasty blow against the side of his face. He raised his arm to his head and the entire room seemed to erupt. A rubber rabbit hit the floor, bounced across the carpet and flung itself at the window. A chair jumped from its corner. Sheets billowed from the bed. Polly was screaming. Matthew Mark Luke Saint John was scrambling into his trousers.

"Get out!" he shouted at Polly. "Get out!" He picked up his shoes, sprinted down the stairs and finished dressing in the street.

Mrs Reynolds stared around the room in dismay. It was a nightmare. She felt humiliated and betrayed. She could accept Matthew Mark Luke Saint John's many crimes of passion but she would never forgive him for stealing the innocence of a child. How she despised him! He had plundered every part of her own body with a loathsome greed, swift and brutal, as the mood took him, at every hour of the day and night, yet still he could not resist a pathetic little morsel like Polly. When she had opened the door, in the confusion of the moment, it had seemed to her astonished eyes that Polly was not trapped, struggling, under the weight of the brute, but had spread herself, swooning, beneath him. It was horrible.

She stared down at the naked pixie. The child looked so

painfully young and brittle. Her arms were thin and her legs were narrow, elbows chipped and knees blue with bruises. It was a miracle that the beast had not killed her in the violence of his attack. Polly, avoiding her mother's eyes, crawled away, folded up her arms and legs and squatted like a spider in a corner of the room. Mrs Reynolds bent and gently wrapped her in a sheet.

"Did he hurt you?" she whispered as she held the child.

"No," sobbed Polly.

"Thank God," muttered Mrs Reynolds. "Did he threaten you? What happened?"

But Polly could not speak. She buried her face in her hands and howled. Mrs Reynolds soaked her in a hot bath and searched discreetly for signs of damage. Polly appeared in the pink of health and this only confirmed her fears that the damage done was soul-deep and beyond repair.

She took the child to her bed. They did not speak but clung to each other and wept themselves to sleep. A chest of drawers, pushed against the door, kept them safe from the sailor. Mrs Reynolds heard him enter the house some time after midnight and stumble slowly up the stairs. He hesitated outside the door but did not try to force himself through the barricade.

She thought he might be bandy with beer. But long after he had gone to his room she lay awake in the dark, too frightened to sleep. It was obvious she had given shelter to a madman. For years she had entertained simple men, stupid men in cheap suits, money in their pockets and beer on their breath. The Hottentot was dangerous. He had taken control of the house and overwhelmed its women. And what did she know about him? He might have come to Rams Horn with secret plans to establish a harem. Tomorrow other women might appear at the door, black women with gold teeth and breasts shaped like cucumbers. He might be a cannibal. Yes, he might be squatting in his room with a bone through his nose, cleaning an axe and dreaming of meat. She thought of his mouth sucking at her flesh, hot grease on his fingers, a bubble of blood on his chin, and she began to cry. The tears rolled into her ears and soaked the pillow. She had to dispose of him before they were murdered in their bed. He had to be removed from the house, packed in a box, pushed from a cliff, thrown into the sea as a meal for the mackerel. And there was only one woman in the town who could help to evict him.

An hour before dawn she woke Polly and helped her dress. As they tiptoed from the room she half-expected the sailor to be lurking in the darkness of the stairs, waiting to leap at them, naked and laughing. But they reached the kitchen in safety and switched on the light.

While she brewed tea and cut a parcel of sandwiches she gave Polly instructions to pedal into the hills and stay away until dusk.

"Why?" demanded Polly. "What am I supposed to do with myself?"

"I don't care," hissed Mrs Reynolds, as she thrust the sandwiches into her daughter's hand. "Break a window. Steal a baby. Set fire to a haystack. Do anything. But stay away from the house."

Polly was puzzled but too frightened to complain. She hurried towards her bicycle.

The first light of morning was already beginning to creep through a crack between the sky and the sea. An early patrol of gulls was sailing in circles beneath the ghost of a stubborn moon. Mrs Reynolds stood on the empty esplanade to watch her daughter escape from sight. And then she locked the house and set out alone for Jamaica Road.

Chapter Seventeen

Mrs Halibut lived alone in her big, stone cottage and the cottage stood alone on Jamaica Road. Many men had tried to leave their boots beneath her bed but none of them had managed it. She didn't care to have a man about the house. She was an independent woman.

She grew her own food and made her own clothes. Cutting sandals from rubber tyres, boiling soap from rabbits or broth from nettles were the simple skills of everyday life for Mrs Halibut. She could skin a rabbit, trap a starling or make glue from chicken quills. There had once been a goat she had kept for its milk but one bad winter she'd eaten it. Her favourite occupation was coaxing the natural medicines from fields and ditches. She could soothe sickness and burn out fever, knit bones and start women bleeding. Fruit pulp for bruises. Cobwebs for scratches. Nothing was wasted.

Mrs Halibut was blessed with the strength of an old martello but she looked as brittle as egg shells. Her hands were small and her face was dainty. She had a long neck, narrow shoulders and fat breasts. Her breasts rolled gently when she walked and pulled at the buttons of her shirt. When she worked in the garden she liked to soak them in sunlight. Whenever she slept she cradled them jealously in her arms. Men wanted to commit unspeakable acts of sex and violence between her breasts. Every night, in Rams Horn bedrooms, her breasts appeared in their dreams. But Mrs Halibut let no man touch them.

One day a man had called at the cottage. He was selling medical dictionaries: *The Home Doctor* and *The Household Nurse*.

"You're a big girl," he said, pushing his suitcase through the door. He rubbed his eyes and grinned. He was staring at Mrs Halibut's breasts. He wanted to bite them, he wanted to skin them and wear them as mittens.

"I don't want anything," said Mrs Halibut as he sat down at the kitchen table.

The salesman laughed. He opened one of the books at Healing Hands and tried to practise Manipulation.

"Don't touch me," warned Mrs Halibut. "The dogs will get jealous."

The salesman laughed again. He stared at her breasts and wiped his tongue around his teeth. He wanted to steal them, he wanted to stuff them and use them as pillows. He opened the second book at Reproduction and read aloud from His Majesty the Male Sex Organ. When he had finished he unbuttoned his trousers and offered a practical demonstration.

Mrs Halibut lowered her eyes. "Would you like a small glass of wine?" she said.

When the salesman woke up he found himself alone in a ditch. His Majesty had been tarred with molasses and wrapped in a jacket of chicken feathers.

Mrs Halibut lived alone and was content. She had no time for men. As caretakers of the world they were greedy, superstitious and violent. As companions for women they were entirely unsuitable. God had made Her one mistake when She had created men.

Chapter Eighteen

The world that morning, yawning in the rising heat, oozing with nectar, creaking with fruit, smelt of fertility, a plump and bursting ripeness. Mrs Reynolds hurried from town, running through the dwindling shadows, towards the safety of the herbalist's cottage. The path was choked with nipplewort and toadflax, thistles and foxgloves. As she kicked through the undergrowth the feathered grass pressed against her skirt and sprayed her legs with seed. Small moths, doped with pollen, flew at her face and fell in flames at her feet. She slapped at the air, cursing, fighting forward, drowning in the rush of sunlight. She ran blind, afraid to glance across her shoulder for fear of finding the naked nigger stalking her with giant strides. She felt his blowtorch breath on her neck, sensed his smell in the nettlebeds, heard his laugh in the cackle of crows.

When she reached the cottage she collapsed on the doorstep and burst into tears. Mrs Halibut came out to help the unhappy woman into the safety of the chintz sitting room and administered cups of sweet, mint tea. For some time Mrs Reynolds could do nothing but cry and snort and wring a handkerchief in her hands. But finally she calmed herself and told the story she had prepared. She told the herbalist about the man in black who had rented her room. He was a darkie. He ate live lobsters, breaking the meat from the claws with his hands. He wouldn't wear shoes and slept on the floor. His feet were filthy, his language obscene and his eyes followed her everywhere.

She suspected he had not previously enjoyed the company of decent, Christian women.

Wrapping her face in the handkerchief and pulling at her nose she explained that, on catching sight of her legs, he had become mad with excitement. And then, with a pantomime of dramatic pauses, rolling eyes and curling fingers, she managed to convey the full range of his carnal appetite, bringing her performance to a dramatic conclusion by bursting into tears again and biting on the handkerchief.

Mrs Halibut was sympathetic. She accepted that Mrs Reynolds might be given to some exaggeration but, nonetheless, she was impressed by the woman's catalogue of miseries.

"How can I help you?" she said.

"I can't throw him out – he's dangerous – he could kill a woman with his bare hands," sobbed Mrs Reynolds.

"Well, I can give you something to help him sleep at night. It's what we call a natural soporific," explained the herbalist.

"Can't you give me something stronger? Something to take away his strength?"

Mrs Halibut shook her head doubtfully. "You would have to mix it with his food. He would suspect something was wrong," she said.

"It doesn't matter. He's a hungry bastard. Perhaps you could find me something to take the edge off his appetite. Something that was so nasty he would be glad to leave me alone."

Mrs Halibut thought for a long time. "Does he eat mushrooms?" she asked casually.

"He'll eat anything."

"Would he recognise a toadstool?"

"He doesn't look at his food and, anyway, he spoils everything with pickle," said Mrs Reynolds in disgust.

"It's dangerous."

"I'll take the risk."

Mrs Halibut frowned and raked her fingers through her hair. She tried to persuade Mrs Reynolds that there were other ways to remove a man. Why, she might easily bury him alive in silence or flay him with jealousy and gossip. But Mrs

Reynolds would have none of them. She had been humiliated by the sailor. He had scratched and scrambled through her underwear, forced her to run naked through her own house, screaming, prised her open and bullied her belly in lewd and violent outbursts of lust and then, most terrible of all, he had thrown her aside in favour of Polly. She would not be content until she had withered his penis and watered his blood.

"I have to think of my daughter," she whispered.

Reluctantly Mrs Halibut went into the kitchen, pulled open the refrigerator door and knelt down to gaze into the sparkling chest of secrets. There, among the bundles of herbs and the necklaces of flowers, beneath the shelves of garlic paste, horse radish, ginseng root and belladonna, in a space alone on the frosty floor, stood a bowl of toadstools. She removed the bowl and carefully chose her poison.

Mrs Halibut loved toadstools. She had a superior knowledge of their qualities and failings. There were the tiny beech sickeners, with their scarlet caps and vague, coconut perfume, that could be used to drown a man in vomit. The humble liberty caps that fired the blood, scrambled the brains and coloured dreams. Fairies' bonnets, stewed in alcohol, were potent enough to knock down a horse and puff-balls, sliced and fried in butter, made an excellent breakfast.

When she returned to the living room she presented her guest with a single, tiny toadstool. Mrs Reynolds held it between finger and thumb and gave it a sniff. She was disappointed. She examined it carefully, rolling it in the palm of her hand. It didn't look dangerous – a shaggy stem plugged by a smooth and innocent cap of flesh – it looked so small and mild she doubted that it would have an effect.

"What is it?" she said, sniffing it again. It had a sweet and sickly odour that tantalized her nose and tried to make her sneeze.

"Amanita Virosa."

"Is it poisonous?"

"Yes," said Mrs Halibut. "It's what we call the destroying angel."

"How do I use it?"

96

"Slice it," said Mrs Halibut. "Mix a slice with a few button mushrooms in a fresh green salad. A little oil and vinegar. A sprinkle of pepper."

"Will it work?"

"Yes, I think he'll want to leave you alone," said Mrs Halibut. She blinked her green eyes and stared at the toadstool.

"It's not very big," Mrs Reynolds complained.

"It's big enough to kill a man," said Mrs Halibut softly.

Mrs Reynolds smiled and wiped her eyes. "Thank you," she said. She slipped the fat petal of poison into the pocket of her skirt and set out again for Rams Horn.

Chapter Nineteen

The big sea boiled, hissed upon the crackling shingle, steamed from the wings of the gulls. The sky roared. On the beach, a yellow newspaper, caught by the furnace draught, began to flutter, scampered, rolled, took flight and sailed high above the town towards the shelter of the hills.

Matthew Mark Luke Saint John was missing when Mrs Reynolds reached home. He had helped himself to a breakfast of eggs and sausage, washed the frying pan, wiped the table, swept the floor and locked the door to his room. Mrs Reynolds retrieved the destroying angel from her skirt and hid it carefully in a corner of the refrigerator. When the sailor returned she would be ready with a welcome of cold beer and toadstool salad.

Alone in the house, she seized the chance to rescue her daughter's clothes and shoes, picture books and one-eyed bear and move them into her own bedroom. They would sleep together now until the African was gone. During the morning she stocked the bedroom fit for a siege – biscuits, fruit and cake in a box, a bottle of brandy under the bed. She tested the bolt on the window and dragged the chest of drawers into position beside the door, ready for the moment when darkness came and they built the barricade. Then she went downstairs to sit and wait for Polly to return.

Dust floated, soft as pollen, in the stagnant air. At noon the heat pressed against the walls of the house, testing the bricks and twisting at the loose rafters. Sunlight pushed through the curtains, cutting the rooms in half with shadow.

At two o'clock the front door rattled and Polly appeared, face freckled and dress crumpled with sweat. Mrs Reynolds, furious with fright, pulled her into the house and scolded her for failing to obey instructions. Why had she come home in the afternoon? She knew it was dangerous. Did she want to be attacked again? Dear God, did she want them both murdered and buried under the floorboards?

"He didn't hurt me," scowled Polly.

"Hasn't he done enough damage?" screamed Mrs Reynolds. But the sight of poor Polly, sprawled sunburnt and exhausted in the hollow of the old sofa, made her anger evaporate.

"We're going to get rid of him," she whispered as she knelt before the sofa. She took Polly's face in her hands and began to drench it with kisses.

"Are you going to send him away tonight?" whispered Polly. Her face collapsed. She stared at her mother and burst into tears.

"Don't cry. He'll soon be gone," promised Mrs Reynolds and rocked the child in her arms.

In the late afternoon gusts of hot sand whirled over the esplanade and scratched a warning at the windows. The shadows in the room crept silently towards the sofa where mother and child lay sleeping. As dusk appeared, Mrs Reynolds woke Polly and retreated to the safety of the bedroom. The shadows grew to fantastic lengths, softened, leaked one into another and filled the town to the chimney pots. The sun rolled slowly into the sea.

Above Rams Horn, moored among the cabbages on the Upton Gabriel Road, Charlie Bloater came on deck to smoke his evening pipe of shag. Somewhere a blackbird was singing. The air still glowed with heat. He smoked and spat and stared at the world until it grew dark and his pipe blew sparks.

Later, wrapped in the twilight, Mrs Halibut locked her cottage and stole as far as the beechwood to collect a purse of belladonna.

When the Dolphin closed, the last to leave were the doctor

and his friend Tom Crow. They strolled into the warm and perfumed night, climbed the cliffs to the Wheel Barrow and sat in the grass to watch for stars in a sky as dark as Guinness. Bats whistled above their heads. Beneath them the town lay shuttered and silent.

At midnight, on Regent Terrace, Mrs Clancy wrapped in silk, opened her bedroom window and beckoned home the spirit of her lost husband before crawling into bed to dream of the ghosts at Fatehpur Sikri. The town sank painfully into sleep.

At one o'clock in the morning a drainpipe creaked in Empire Road, a cat hissed, and Vernie Stringer fell into the street. He hit the cobbles with a gasp, somersaulted and lay motionless, stretched like a broken albatross in the gutter. A moment later Smudger ran from a doorway and helped him to his feet.

"Did you bring a torch?" whispered Vernie, nursing his elbows.

"Yes," whispered Smudger. He pulled a bag from his shirt and flourished a long rubber torch. When he pressed the button a spear of yellow light sprang from his hand and pinned Vernie's plimsolls to the cobbles.

"And the masks!" prompted Vernie. "You didn't forget the masks?"

Smudger pulled a pair of his mother's stockings from the bag. He had stolen them from the laundry basket and spent most of the afternoon cutting and knotting them into shape.

"They're enormous," complained Vernie as they hurried down the street.

"No," said Smudger. "I worked on them so they fit perfect."

He pulled a mask over his head. He had fashioned crude slits for the eyes. The foot dangled from the top of his skull like a nipple.

"Jesus, you look horrible!" whispered Vernie with an admiring glance. He struggled to fit his own mask.

They ran on tiptoe through the phantom town, alarmed by the silence, the empty streets, the narrow houses planted in rows like tombstones. It was like this when you were dead. Perhaps they would *meet* the dead in the next street, rising up

100

from Hell through the drains, shuffling towards them with stinking flesh and foaming faces.

"I hope she drank her Bournvita," whispered Smudger.

"Nothing can go wrong," promised Vernie. It was a night of miracles. They were loose in the town and before them Sickly's mother lay waiting, shackled by sleep to her great feather bed. He thought of her curled with her head pushed under the pillows and her bum stuck out through the sheets. They could do anything. They could feast on her glorious, unfrocked fat, thumb her tits, squeeze her snapper, bite her bum; while she, with her eyes closed and legs open, would know nothing.

He touched the blades of the kitchen scissors he had hidden in his pocket. The blood sang in his ears. It was a night of miracles.

"I hate it," said Smudger as they ran down the Parade towards the esplanade.

"What?" whispered Vernie.

"Bournvita," said Smudger. He shivered when he heard the sea. It seemed to rumble in the darkness as if it might, at any moment, flood the beach and drown the streets. He stared out towards Whelk Pier. His mouth was dry. His blue eyes grown as hard as marbles. They turned and ran towards Lantern Street.

When they reached Sickly's garden they squatted in the bushes to watch the house. Old George was wheezing peacefully in one of the dusty flowerbeds. The dark air was scented with honeysuckle.

"Give him the signal," whispered Vernie.

Smudger took aim with the torch and stabbed the button. Three short bursts of light flashed across the lawn and tapped on the kitchen window.

"He's fallen asleep," hissed Vernie impatiently.

"No," said Smudger. "He'll be there."

They crouched in the bushes, hardly daring to breathe, until at last the kitchen window swung open and Sickly appeared, a luminous dwarf in crumpled pyjamas, waving at them to approach.

"You'll have to climb through the window. I don't know how to unlock the door," he called out in a hoarse whisper as they scampered across the lawn. Vernie made a sprint at the open window and vaulted neatly into the kitchen.

"Did the tablets work?" he demanded as he turned to help drag Smudger aboard.

"Yes," said Sickly.

"Is she asleep?" said Smudger, staring around the kitchen gloom.

"Yes, snoring like a pig," said Sickly.

Smudger grinned and scratched his ears through the stocking mask. He saw Sickly's mother as a huge porker rolled in straw, ears loose, trotters stiff, her pink belly hot and steaming.

"Let's go," said Vernie.

"I'm not coming with you," said Sickly.

"Why?" demanded Smudger suspiciously.

"I don't know," said Sickly. "I don't want to look." He wiped his nose on his sleeve.

"You're scared."

"I've seen it," he reminded them, scornfully. He turned away. His feet pattered towards the door.

"Where are you going?' said Smudger, flashing his torch in Sickly's direction.

"I'm going back to bed. When you've had a look you can get out again through the window," he said and disappeared.

"We don't need him," sneered Vernie. He felt confident now they were inside the house and he trusted the power of the sleeping tablets. Sickly's mother was already their prisoner. His own mother had fallen out of bed while under the influence and spent the rest of the night asleep on the carpet. It was strong medicine.

They crept upstairs by the light of the torch and into the forbidden bedroom. Smudger swung the torch beam over the wardrobe, along the floor and found the bottom of the bed.

"Jesus," gasped Vernie. His eyes blazed like bonfires. His ears smouldered. He thought his head would explode. Sickly's mother lay asleep in the bed. She was sleeping naked because

102

of the heat and one of her legs had slipped through the sheets and glowed, soft and pale, in the torchlight.

He stared at the leg for a long time. It was so lovely he wanted to scream. The narrow beam of light licked across the heel of the foot, over the knee and settled on the swelling thigh. It was so lovely he wanted to throw his arms around the wicked curve of it, shake it, squeeze it, sink his teeth in the plump and smothering softness.

"Pull down the sheets," whispered Smudger from the safety of the door. He rubbed at his face through the mask. The stocking stung like nettles.

Vernie crept towards the bed and hesitated. "Hold the light," he gasped. "I can't see nothing."

The torchlight flashed, danced against the wall and settled again upon the sleeping woman. Her face was buried in pillow and she whistled softly as she breathed. A strand of damp hair curled against the edge of her mouth. Vernie flexed his fingers, stretched out a hand and gently, very gently, drew down the sheet. She was sleeping slightly twisted, with her arm concealing her breasts. She smelt of carnations, burnt sugar and hot sultana cake.

"Pull out her tits," croaked Smudger. He was clutching the torch with both hands, holding it at arm's length, trying to control the trembling beam of light. It had worked! He couldn't believe it. She was there on the bed in the stark, staring, snapper-screaming nude!

Mercy Peters opened her eyes and peered blindly around the room. "What is it?" she moaned, still stupid with sleep.

"Nothing," whispered Vernie.

"What's happening?" she roared, clutching at the sheet and leaping, startled, from the mattress.

"We were looking for the dog," squealed Smudger. He turned to run but his rubbery legs sent him spinning in circles. In the confusion the woman snatched the torch and trapped the outlaws in a corner. The sheet had fallen from her shoulders and she stood, tall and naked, before them. But Vernie and Smudger crouched, dazzled by light, and hid their faces in their hands.

103

"We thought you were asleep," stammered Vernie. His teeth chattered with fright.

Mercy Peters glared at him. Her buttocks quivered with rage. She swung the torch like a truncheon, catching him against the side of the head and knocking him against the wall. He howled with fright, staggered back through the door, fell over his feet and rolled down the stairs with his head between his knees. Smudger flew behind him. His stocking was torn and his nose was bleeding.

"We were looking for the dog," sobbed Vernie, clutching his ears.

Mercy Peters thundered barefoot down the stairs and chased them into the kitchen. She made a grab for the smallest one, caught him by the collar and tried to hold him. But he wriggled from her grasp, shot through the window and followed Vernie into the garden where Old George was waiting with bleary eyes and poisonous fangs. In the darkness of the kitchen Mercy Peters stood and screamed. Her breasts were wet with tiny, rolling beads of blood.

Chapter Twenty

That night the doctor dreamed of Mrs Clancy. She was sitting, half-naked, in the draughty waiting room. She wore black stockings and black leather shoes, a pair of black gloves and a long, black veil. She sat silent with her spine erect and her hands folded into her lap. Her hair was loose. Her arms smelt of gardenias.

After a long time a bell rang. The widow stood up and walked into the empty surgery. Her shoes clicked on the stone floor. The stockings whispered around her thighs.

The doctor recognised the desk, the bed, the medicine box and the big, folding screens. There were the magazines where he had thrown them. There were his boots and his raincoat. But something was different. Something was changed. The metal bed had been placed in the centre of the room. There was a sheet thrown over the bed and beneath the sheet a corpse.

Mrs Clancy stood beside the bed, pulled at the sheet and let it fall, gasping, around her feet. When the doctor found the courage to look at the body he met his own face staring back at him. He was naked. His eyes were open. His hands were crossed upon his chest and his ankles were tied together with string.

Then he saw Mrs Clancy lift her veil and stare at the corpse. Her face was white but her mouth was crimson. There were tears, small as sequins, glinting in her narrowed eyes.

She bent to the corpse and kissed it, her lips staining the smooth, cold skin. She reached down and pressed shut the eyes with her fingertips. She turned and walked away.

He wanted to rise from the dead and return her embrace. He wanted to open his eyes and scream. But it was too late. He could not lift himself from the bed. When he woke up Mrs Clancy had gone and his head was wrapped in a pillow.

Chapter Twenty-One

"I don't understand it," scowled Smudger as he picked his nose. They were sitting in the safety of their bunker beneath the giant beech tree. Above them the afternoon was a suffocating fog of heat and dust.

"He didn't use them," said Vernie bitterly and nursed his head in his hands. His ears were swollen and there were long, scarlet scratches on his face. He'd been lucky to escape the suspicions of his mother – at breakfast she had been too busy soaking the bandages from her legs to notice his wounds – but when he went home tonight he would have to claim he'd been fighting with Smudger.

"Why?" said Smudger. "Why didn't he use 'em? He only had to stick 'em in her Bournvita."

"It's obvious," said Vernie impatiently. "He *wanted* us to get caught."

"We might have been arrested," said Smudger, wiping his finger on his shirt.

"We might have got killed," complained Vernie.

They sank into silence, depressed by the heat and the pain of defeat. After a while Vernie tried farting, a sharp, sweet cracker of a fart, but they found no pleasure in it. Smudger tried to revive his own spirits by conjuring up the shape of Sickly's nude mother, jumping from bed, frozen for a second in the beam of his torch. His eyes had taken the photograph but his memory refused to develop the picture. There was nothing but noise and fear and darkness.

"Did you see anything?" he asked hopefully, as he glanced at Vernie.

"No, she was too quick," said Vernie.

They slipped again into silence. Smudger peered around the gloomy cave and wondered how long they would have to hide. Polly had promised he could have a feel for fifty pence. She hadn't explained what parts of her body were available at that price. But it was better than nothing. Where would he find fifty pence? And how would he meet her without getting caught? They couldn't walk the streets in safety until Sickly's mother had forgotten them and that might take months.

"I'm going to kill him," said Vernie softly.

"It's no good. He'd tell his mother and then she'd call the police," said Smudger. He had expected the police to arrive the moment he had opened his eyes that morning. He thought they would be standing at the foot of the bed waiting for him. He couldn't understand why they had failed to arrest him.

"He won't be talking to anyone when I've finished," promised Vernie.

"What are you going to do to him?"

"He's going to have an accident."

"You could get Frank's big brother to help. He put someone in hospital last year for smiling at his girlfriend," said Smudger. And it was true. Frank's brother was a vicious sod. He'd spit at you for looking at him. He'd break your legs for stepping on his shadow in the street.

"No," grumbled Vernie. "We don't want nobody to know about it. We've got to make it look like a proper accident." He took out his penknife and began to cut a little picture on the wall of the cave. A simple circle for a face and a fat, sausage body. It was a portrait of Sickly's wonderful mother. He added arms and legs and a scrawl of hair.

"He could fall through the pier," Smudger suggested helpfully. "The boards are rotten and slippery when it rains."

"Yes, and he can't swim," said Vernie with a ghostly smile. He drew the breasts, long balloons of joy that fastened under the arms like a pair of angel's wings.

"Or he could disappear out there on the mudflats," said

108

Smudger, jerking his head in the general direction of the Sheep.

"They find skeletons in the mud sometimes," Vernie said thoughtfully.

"We warned him," said Smudger.

"That's right," said Vernie.

"We gave him every chance," said Smudger.

"Plenty," said Vernie. "And now it's too late." He began to work on the magic snapper, the penknife held by the tip of its blade, scribbling a beard at the base of the sausage.

Smudger stared at Vernie. His mouth fell open. The truth flared in his head like a maroon.

"Are you serious?" he whispered.

Vernie nodded. His face was grey. His ears looked black. He frowned at the picture on the wall and scratched it out with his knife.

Chapter Twenty-Two

Matthew Mark Luke Saint John came strolling down the esplanade with his hands in his pockets and sand in his shoes. He had slept rough for two nights – penance enough for an hour's rough-riding with Polly – and now he was coming home. He whistled through his teeth as he walked to the house with the crooked red door. The key was warm in his pocket.

On the first evening, after hiding in the hills, he had gone down to sleep on the beach. Under cover of darkness he had buried himself to the neck in a shallow grave of sand and quietly stared at the stars. He was worried that Mrs Reynolds had discovered him playing with her daughter but he had no doubts she would forgive him. He wanted both of them. It was wrong to have favourites among women. In Tangier he had seen a sailor disembowelled by a jealous woman. She had split his stomach with a razor and the tripe fell out on the floor. It was terrible. The woman screaming. The tripe steaming. He had never forgotten it. But a mother should be proud to share a man with her daughter. They were the same flesh, they grew on the same branch, the one fruit green and the one fruit ripe. Mrs Reynolds was soft and loose and leaked syrup when he squeezed her with his thumbs. Polly was small and hard and her skin tasted bitter between his teeth. How could a man be expected to choose between them? The thought of the two women stirred him so much that he brushed the sand from his trouser buttons and waved his stick at the stars.

At dawn he had left the beach and walked as far as the Upton Gabriel Road to join Charlie Bloater for breakfast. They spent the day talking of coasters, cargoes and fishing fleets. Charlie said that next year he was going to leave the cabbages and set sail for the Pacific Islands, Fiji, Samoa and Tonga where, they said, men never worked and women danced naked at night. Matthew Mark Luke Saint John said he'd heard of such places in Liverpool. Later they sank a gallon of cider and then, too drunk to climb aboard the boat, had slept among the cabbages.

Now he had come home. He pulled the key from his pocket and unlocked the door. The hall was empty. The bicycle was missing. Polly had been sent out to buy bread and bacon. He sniffed at the cool, comforting smells of lavender floor polish, fresh linen and cut roses, strolled across the hall and paused to knock his knuckles against the barometer.

At the rattle of the front door, Mrs Reynolds, anxious for the girl to come home safely from her errand, ran downstairs in her underwear.

"Good morning," he said, his eyes moist as raisins as he watched her make the descent. She had painted her toenails. Her bare legs shone. Her pants were trimmed with a little beard of lace.

Mrs Reynolds screamed, skidded across the floor and ran into the parlour. When he followed her into the room he found her kneeling behind the sofa.

"Don't touch me!" she screeched. She grabbed a cushion and pressed it against her stomach. The stiff, silver cones of her brassiere, peeking through the cushion, looked as sharp as beaks.

"It's going to be another hot day," the sailor said gently, glancing through the window.

Mrs Reynolds scrambled to the window and peered nervously across the esplanade. She had dreamt he would return with a press-gang of ebony sailors, mad with rum and the promise of women. Swooning under a chloroformed hood, she'd been carried away and had woken to find herself hanging in chains on a boat in the South China Sea. But the esplanade was empty.

111

"I'll scream!" she threatened.

He smiled. In her excitement she had dented one of the cones. He wanted to reach out and pinch it back into shape, bite off the end with his teeth and gently tease the nipple through the torn cotton. But he turned, instead, and stared at his feet.

"I think I'll change my shoes."

"Touch Polly and I'll kill you," she bellowed as he walked away and went upstairs to his room. She didn't know whether to follow him or run, screaming, into the street. She had expected to be tied to a chair and flogged. She had expected to be seized and gnawed like a ham bone. She threw the cushion at the wall.

Matthew Mark Luke Saint John stayed in his room for the rest of the day. He read the bible and fell asleep. When he approached Mrs Reynolds again he found her working with Polly in the kitchen. It was getting dark. The table was buried under piles of tomatoes, mushrooms, radishes, cucumbers, thick sticks of celery and heaps of damp lettuce. The evening air was scented with the sweet sting of onions.

"Have you seen the newspaper?" he inquired from a respectable distance. He cocked his head and stared around the room like an old fox inspecting a chicken coop.

"I threw it away," snapped Mrs Reynolds, wiping her hands on her apron and scowling at him. She picked up a knife and held it lightly in her fist.

"That's a pity," sighed the sailor.

Polly was circumcising a cucumber. She glanced up at him and blushed. The tips of her ears glowed scarlet through a web of dusty curls.

"Are you hungry?" asked Mrs Reynolds as he turned to walk away.

"Yes," he said. He watched her plunge her hand into a bucket of boiled prawns, pull one out by its whiskers and crack off its head.

"Go and sit down," she said.

Matthew Mark Luke Saint John sat in the dining room and obediently waited for his supper. A few minutes later he was presented with a huge bowl of vegetables, sliced, chopped, torn and grated, spiked with prawns and tossed in olive oil. Mrs Reynolds ate a pepper and tomato sandwich. Polly picked at a slice of cheese. They watched the sailor eat in silence, their eyes following the fork as it prodded, stabbed and carried each morsel into the giant's mouth.

At last he pushed the bowl away and began picking his teeth with a fingernail. Mrs Reynolds stared at the empty bowl. She blinked her grey eyes and shivered. The sailor grinned and sucked at a stubborn shred of prawn held fast in a hollow molar. He knew now that he had been forgiven his trespasses. He understood women. They might fight and struggle but they all loved to feel the slap of the mattress. Mrs Reynolds had prepared this supper as a gesture of love. Tonight she might even spread her buttocks for him. The thought made him chuckle with pleasure. He would take a bath and wait for her to come to his room.

"You were going to send him away," hissed Polly when the sailor had gone.

"Patience," muttered Mrs Reynolds.

"Can I sleep in my own bed tonight?" Polly pleaded as they cleared the remains of the meal.

"No."

"He wouldn't do it *again*!" said Polly, her face as pink as a peony.

"He's cunning – he'd try anything," warned Mrs Reynolds. She sniffed suspiciously at the sailor's bowl as she carred it into the kitchen.

They reached the safety of their bedroom while Matthew Mark Luke Saint John was still splashing in the bath. Polly quickly fell asleep, exhausted by excitement. But Mrs Reynolds lay awake in the dark and waited for the flutter of wings, the kiss of death, the moment when her destroying angel folded the sailor into its poisoned embrace.

At six o'clock in the morning she heard a terrible bellow of pain that shook the bed and made the dust dance in the floorboards. She was so frightened that she held her breath, went cold as a corpse and pulled the sheet across her face. The bellow was followed by a deep, rumbling growl of anger and the slap of bare feet as the sailor ran to the bathroom.

Mrs Reynolds scrambled to the bedroom door and peered through the keyhole. There was another shout of pain and then the sound of soup hitting a bucket.

"What's happening?" cried Polly.

"It's him," whispered Mrs Reynolds. "I think he's having some sort of attack."

There was a gasp, a cough, a few words of Pidgin, and then a queer rattling noise like a man running in circles on his hands and knees.

"Help him!" screeched Polly. She was standing on the bed and screaming with fright. Her face was white. The hair coiled in snakes around her neck.

Mrs Reynolds dragged the chest of drawers away from the door and ran into the bathroom. Matthew Mark Luke Saint John was squatting, naked, on the floor. A thick, hot gravy spurted from his mouth and nose.

"Me sik-man," he gurgled, blindly rolling his eyes. "Chit!" His face sagged like a sack of coal.

She stood and watched in horror as he gave a sudden shout and rolled across the floor with his fingers clutching his stomach. The gravy glistened on his shoulders.

"Ah, me belly e de hot," he gasped. "Jezous-Cres, me belly e de hot!"

Mrs Reynolds tried to grab his ears and push his head into the bath. It was horrible. He struggled and coughed and sprayed her feet. He seemed to be leaking from every hole in his body. Mrs Clancy's demon king was melting into a poisonous puddle.

Polly crept into the bathroom and hid behind her mother's dressing-gown.

"Dis ouman e bad plenti," he shouted, wagging his head at the girl.

He tried to stagger to his feet but fell against the mirror and slithered down the wall.

"Kouik! Kouik!" he pleaded. "Sakramen for sik-man." He blew a bubble and collapsed in the stinking gravy.

114

"Polly, fetch the doctor!" cried Mrs Reynolds.

But Polly was already down the stairs and pushing her bicycle into the street.

Chapter Twenty-Three

The doctor was asleep when Polly spun her bicycle into Storks Yard. She threw herself against the surgery door and banged the bell with her fist. It was still dark in the yard. A thin, cold mist curled from the cobbles and swirled against her bare ankles. She wore sandals and a dressing-gown. There had been no time to waste on clothes. She punched and kicked at the door until, at last, the doctor leaned from the bedroom window. His face was yellow and his eyes were pink with sleep. He had been dreaming again of Mrs Clancy.

"What's wrong?" he mumbled, rubbing his head with his hand.

"Quick! He's having an attack!" Polly panted.

"Where?" shouted the baffled doctor, staring about the yard.

"All over the bathroom," gasped Polly, skipping with excitement.

He ran downstairs to unchain the door. It was his first emergency call for months. He grabbed an overcoat to cover his pyjamas and went running in search of shoes. He lost the key to the medicine cabinet and dropped his wristwatch on the floor.

"Don't get excited!" he yelled to Polly as he ran from room to room. "We'll save him."

While the doctor went to collect his bag Polly peeped into the waiting room and glanced nervously at the line of dark and dusty wooden chairs. She was scared of the mysterious, evil-smelling surgery where, it was rumoured, they took you for examinations. Brenda Butler said they pulled down your pants and forced you flat on a metal bed and used a shoe horn to pull you open and stare at you with a torch disguised as a fountain pen. Brenda Butler had gone to a doctor in Drizzle and he had made her undress and then fiddled with her until it hurt and squeezed her breasts and forced her to piddle in a pot. It was shocking. Brenda had kept it a secret for weeks because her mother would have murdered her if she'd known. But Polly liked Doctor Douglas – he was a big, foolish brute of a man with enormous paws and a crumpled smile. She felt safe enough with him.

The doctor rushed from the surgery and chased Polly into the yard.

"You get home and I'll follow," he instructed.

Polly leapt astride her bicycle, kicked the pedals and vanished through an arch of sunlight.

The doctor pushed the heavy leather bag under his arm and sprinted from Storks Yard. He ran across the high street, along the length of Albert Road, down Regent Terrace and limped onto the esplanade.

Mrs Reynolds was standing on her doorstep, waving her arms like a drowning woman. She had managed to wash down the sailor with a kettle of water and help him back to bed. He looked ghastly but he had stopped leaking and his English had improved. She had splashed the bathroom with Dettol.

"Are you the doctor?" whispered Matthew Mark Luke Saint John as the doctor tiptoed into the room.

"Yes," said the doctor, staring at the mound of bedclothes.

The giant pulled the sheets from his face and glanced quickly about the room. "Poison," he whispered. "She tried to poison me."

"Mrs Reynolds?"

"Yes," said the sailor.

"Well, let's have a look at you," the doctor said cheerfully, sitting down on the edge of the bed.

"That's a nasty cut above your eye," he said as he noticed the groove the hairbrush had made in the sailor's eyebrow.

"She tried to put out my eyes," moaned the sailor.

"Mrs Reynolds?"

"Yes."

The doctor smiled at the thought of this giant buffalo living in fear of a little sparrow like Mrs Reynolds. But it was an ugly wound. He had probably fallen, drunk, and cracked his head on the pavement.

"She sounds like a dangerous woman."

"Wicked."

"You'll have to behave yourself," grinned the doctor.

He finished the examination in silence, felt the sailor's pulse and peered at his tongue, poked his stomach and gave him a friendly slap on the back.

"What have you eaten in the last twenty-four hours?" he said at last, kneeling to open his battered bag of tricks.

"Prawns. A big plate of prawns," whispered Matthew Mark Luke Saint John. "Full of poison," he added bitterly.

The doctor struggled through the jumble of dressings and syringes, pessaries and strappings. "Did anyone else eat prawns?" he said as he pulled out a bottle of Milk of Magnesia.

"No," barked the sailor impatiently. "They were poisoned."

"Well, I think you're through the worst of it. I'll give you something to settle your stomach. Stay in bed. Eat nothing. Read the instructions." He placed the Milk of Magnesia on the bedside table.

"You've got to help me," pleaded the sailor. He was sweating. His face shone. His hair glittered like a skull cap of beads.

"You'll be fine. I know prawns can be nasty," said the doctor gently. "Some people can't touch them. But you're not in danger . . ."

"You don't hear what I'm telling you. She's trying to kill me. She poisoned the prawns," said the sailor. His eyes were swollen. A pearl of sweat hung, wobbling, from the end of his nose.

"I don't understand."

"I need protection. I need something to protect me from

118

her spells," whispered the sailor. He pulled anxiously at the doctor's sleeve and dragged him back to the bed.

"You want me to protect you from poor Mrs Reynolds?"

"She cast a spell on the prawns," whispered the sailor.

"Why?"

"She's a jealous woman," said the sailor. "She'd like to see me locked away." His eyebrows twitched, his eyes bulged and he began to giggle. It was a crazy warble of laughter that shook his shoulders and rattled the bed.

The doctor frowned. "I'll give you some tablets," he said, scratching again in his bag. He found a bottle of Valium and shook half a dozen of them into his hand.

"What are these?"

"Diazepam," said the doctor. "Take one before you eat your meals."

"Will they protect me?"

"Yes," smiled the doctor. "They work like magic."

"Sing to Jesus," sighed the sailor and closed his eyes.

"What's wrong with him, doctor? Is it something tropical?" asked Mrs Reynolds when the doctor had finished in the bedroom.

"Food poisoning."

"Oh, how dreadful!" she shouted, wringing her hands. "I don't know how it could have happened. I'm always so careful with his food and he gets the best of everything. Plenty of fresh fruit and raw vegetables . . ." She had slipped into a clean frock ready for her interrogation and arrest. There were paper hankies in her handbag and a change of underwear.

"Prawns?"

"Oh, yes. Prawns. Lobsters. Crabs," she boasted.

"You can't trust shellfish in this weather," he said, shaking his head.

"Does he think I gave him bad prawns?"

"He's a little confused," said the doctor. "He thinks you're plotting to get rid of him."

Mrs Reynolds swayed dangerously and sat down in a chair. "Is he going to die?" she whispered. She had used no more than a slice of angel. She hadn't meant to kill him. God knows,

119

she didn't want to see him dead. But the sailor had nearly disintegrated in the bathroom.

"Don't worry," laughed the doctor. "He's upset and a long way from home. He's just feeling a little sorry for himself at the moment."

Mrs Reynolds sat and stared at the doctor with her mouth open. She nodded, yes, thank God, a lot of shouting about nothing, a nasty smell, but no harm done. She felt bewildered by the verdict. She thought there must be some mistake.

"I've given him some Milk of Magnesia for the comfort of his stomach and a few Valium to try and calm him down," he explained. He paused to smile at Mrs Reynolds. He was flattered she had sent for him and not called out the herbalist; although he didn't understand it. There was so much he didn't understand. "Is there anything else?" he inquired, reaching out to squeeze her hand.

"No, thank you," she said absently.

"Does he drink?" asked the doctor, snapping the locks on his leather bag.

"How did you know?" gasped Mrs Reynolds, as if a scandal had been uncovered.

The doctor shrugged and smiled. "I'm a doctor," he said as he turned to leave the room.

Chapter Twenty-Four

Matthew Mark Luke Saint John sat in bed and stared at the tablets nesting in the palm of his hand. They worked like magic, those were the doctor's words, and the doctor had no reason to cheat him. Here was magic that could protect him from the mortal effects of witchcraft and poison. He remembered the tribesmen he had seen as a child in Victoria, the men from the North, who could tread hot coals and cast out demons. He had seen these things with his own eyes. And now, without warning, in the darkness of defeat, he had been given the power to eat glass, swallow razor blades and suck the venom from snakes.

He glared around the room. He was tired of the rosebud wallpaper and the narrow grave of a bed. He was tired of Mrs Reynolds with her jealous rage and her pasty, uncooked body. Jesus had granted each man a gift – his own gift was prodigious – and he could not allow one woman, alone, to hide it under her bushel. She would live to regret this piddling plot to kill him. He would have his revenge. He would strike true terror into her pagan, superstitious heart.

He rattled the tablets in his fist and chuckled. The drug could fetch a high price on the black market. The Chinese gave gold for a pinch of smuggled rhino horn. They would give a king's ransom to own a remedy for poison. He would use the money to buy opium from the poppy fields of Turkey, trade the opium in Germany for American pornography, enough to fill a boat, trade the filth in Egypt for Kalashnikov AK-47 assault rifles and sell the weapons to the madman in Marseilles. And then, when he was rich, he would go back home and build a bordello.

He had seen the dance halls of Douala, the little Frenchmen strutting drunk and the women mocking them with laughter. The women only stirred those passions they knew the beer would extinguish. At night, through the chinks in the iron shutters, he had watched from the street as the women danced, the men fell down and the money rolled on the dusty floor. He would build a *real* bordello with a grand staircase and air-conditioned bedrooms. It would be a brothel as big and bumptious as any pleasure palace in the world. The walls would be curtained with antique carpets and the doors would be carved from Burmese teak. He would find slender, high-breasted Kirdi women, dress them in bracelets of pierced centimes and rub their skins with pineapple juice. He would entertain film stars, presidents and princes. His suits would be silk and his teeth would be silver. He would eat truffles and sleep in a bed made from elephant tusks.

He sat and counted his riches while the pain in his belly continued to smoulder. His throat hurt and his lungs were raw. He read the bible for comfort and slept through the heat of the afternoon. He dreamt of naked Kirdi women softly crooning his favourite hymns as they danced a circle around him. When he woke he dressed painfully, wrapped the precious tablets in little twists of paper and tucked them into his boots. Then he opened the window and let the smell of warm mud and seaweed gust through the room. It was time to return to the sea.

At sunset he picked up his suitcase and, without a word to Mrs Reynolds, without so much as a glance at Polly, walked from the house and disappeared into the dusk at the end of the empty esplanade.

"Is he going home?" asked Polly in alarm, as she ran to the window and watched the giant fade away.

"Yes."

"Why?" moaned Polly. "Why?"

122

"That's what happens with men – when they've finished with you they just walk away," sneered Mrs Reynolds.

"But he could die out there," Polly sobbed. She couldn't believe that Matthew Mark Luke Saint John would leave her alone with her mother. It was wrong. He had promised to take her home with him. She was going to escape from Rams Horn. They were going to live on bananas and honey and sleep in the top of a tree. They had planned everything. He wouldn't walk away without leaving her instructions to follow. There must be something wrong. "He needs help," she cried, pressing her face against the window, smearing the glass with tears.

"Rubbish! There's nothing wrong with him."

"The doctor said he was poisoned!" shouted Polly. She had her suspicions about the sailor's last supper.

"Men! They'll do anything to try and pull the sheets over your eyes. You can't trust them as far as you can spit. Remember what happened when I left him alone in the house? He might have killed you if I hadn't caught him."

"He didn't hurt me," protested Polly.

"You're a child!" snapped Mrs Reynolds impatiently and slapped Polly's ear.

Polly screamed and threw a tantrum. She was old enough to understand. She was old enough to run away and follow him. She threatened murder. She threatened suicide. She threatened to be sick. But she knew it was hopeless. The sailor had gone.

The next morning Mrs Reynolds cleaned the house. She swept from room to room, tore down the barricades and bombed the bathroom with bleach. She attacked the sailor's room in a fury of bristles and soap suds, thrashed the curtains and beat the carpet.

While her mother worked, Polly crept to her own bedroom and frantically searched for some hidden message from the mariner. He might have written something in the dust beneath her bed or tucked a scrap of paper under her pillows. He must have left something. Yet despite pulling the room apart she could find no trace of him.

Chapter Twenty-Five

Mrs Reynolds found the doll. It was hidden in the sailor's wardrobe. At first she thought it was a lost dishcloth, long forgotten and dried in the shape of withered cabbage. But when she pulled it from its hiding place and turned it over in her hands she saw an ugly matchbox face, two seashell breasts and, tucked beneath the dangling belly, a little beard of human hair. And then, with a shiver of disgust, she recognised Polly! The doll was made, not from rag, but from one of Polly's winter gloves, stolen from the child's wardrobe. It was Polly's hair, knotted and stitched beneath the doll's belly. She was holding an obscene and clumsy effigy of her own daughter!

She threw the doll upon the bed and waved her hands in terror. It fell with a plop on the pillow and sat, stiff as a cockroach, waiting to spring into life. She wanted to pull off her shoes and beat the puppet to death. Smash the shells. Pull out the hair. Crush the hollow matchbox head. But this was the Devil's needlework. She couldn't fight the Devil. Mrs Clancy had warned her they would need a priest. And it was true. She could not destroy the doll for fear that a little of Polly's soul had already been forced into transmigration and lay trapped in the crumpled effigy. And, while the doll existed, she knew that Polly was in constant danger since the sailor might have fashioned two dolls from the gloves and carried the sister away with him, hoping to work his mischief by transmitting some diabolical sorcery, one to the other, from the safety of his hiding place.

She knelt down beside the bed and fixed her eyes on the pillow. Was it possible to draw the power from the doll and render it harmless? If she buried the doll, would Polly smother in her sleep? If she burned it, would Polly burn with an unholy fever? What would happen if she made a doll in the image of the sailor? Would it work? How? Should she pray? When? The questions swarmed in her head without answer. Our Father who art in Heaven. She felt tired and lonely and old.

At last she managed to pick up the pillow and carried the doll, like a crown upon a cushion, to the empty wardrobe. Then she locked the door, slipped the key beneath the carpet and ran from the room. And so the sailor continued to haunt the house, throwing his shadow across their lives, waiting his moment to snatch at Polly.

Chapter Twenty-Six

The darkness spreads from the sea at Rams Horn and creeps among the cobbled streets. The houses fade from their roots to their rafters. Dogs become shadows, trotting home from the lost, grey beach. At dusk small boys and old men are deprived of their clothes and dumped in the bath while women complain and clatter in kitchens. Kettles thunder, pipes bubble and the smell of fried sausage hangs in the courtyards. Later, when all the curtains have been drawn, the women yawn and settle down to soak in the soft blue, lonely, television light. And then there is silence. The streets have gone. The town shrinks between black hills. The sea gropes for the shore.

But out of the darkness on Pilgrim Street the Dolphin burns like a bonfire; its windows blaze and the rooms are filled with smoke. Tonight Big Lily White bellows abuse as he wrestles with a constipated beer engine, Oswald Murdoch weeps with the whisky and Tanner Atkins juggles with glasses. A farmer from Drizzle drinks until his braces snap, jumps up and dances to the music playing in his head. An old sailor from the Dreadnought Buildings sucks a dirge from a bent harmonica and the men of the Dolphin start to sing. They sing and argue and fight together until Big Lily White grows tired of the noise and turns his customers into the night.

When the floors have been swept and the beer pumps polished, Tanner Atkins pulls off his apron and sits at a table to comb his hair. He blows his nose and winds his wristwatch.

It is twenty minutes to midnight. He feels tired but he will not sleep. He drags his bicycle into the street, waves goodbye to the weary landlord and whispers out on the phantom patrol. Away he pedals with his shirt-tails flying and his cap pulled over his ears. An old man on a rusting Raleigh. But on the corner of Pilgrim Street he is transformed. He shrinks to the size of a goblin. His skin turns transparent. His eyes grow bright as headlamps. He becomes a wolf. A magic tiger. The sultan of Rams Horn. The fabulous philanderer.

Along the Parade he buries his bicycle in the bushes and stops to stare, through a crack in the shutter, at Rosie Stunts, the grocer's daughter, counting biscuits in her sleep. Fig rolls and coconut fancies. Rich tea and small digestives. He watches her fumble from shelf to shelf, her bum ballooning through striped pyjamas, the biscuits crunching beneath her feet. The window steams. The keyhole whistles. Look out, Rosie, here's Tanner Atkins, come to suck on your chocolate fingers.

Behind Anchor Street he throws back his head to test the warm and salty darkness. His eyes jump from their sockets, sprout wings and circle the rooftops, searching out chinks in bedroom curtains. Flying over the quiet town they settle, at last, in Jamaica Road where, secret in the cottage kitchen, Mrs Halibut kneels at a basin, sponging her breasts by candlelight. The water glows. The sponge pulls at the dripping nipples. Tanner Atkins, disguised as a fruit bush, leans against the lattice window. He gawks and goggles, squints and sniggers, bares his teeth and grins like a dog.

All night he rides through the perfumed shadows, smudging windows, raiding keyholes. Here's little Doris, the plumber's wife, sipping milk to soothe a nightmare, climbing stairs without her knickers. There's Ivy Murdoch, through the curtains, fat thighs pinched in new silk stockings, strutting about in the butcher's apron. Tanner moans and his face turns black. His heart bursts like a worn-out corset.

At last, spinning down through a path in the cliffs, he rolls his bicycle into the sand and creeps as far as Tom Crow's cottage. It is almost dawn. Smoke drifts from the rusting funnel. A rat goes running between his feet. In the cottage

127

garden Tanner scoops a nest from the seaweed and sits to wait for the idiot girl. For a long time he sits there, warming his mouth with peppermint balls. He sits so long that his old knees crack and a chill from the sea makes his whiskers bristle. And then, when his hope has nearly gone and he starts to dream of a hot bed and breakfast, the girl appears at the cottage door.

Mad-eyed and grinning, wrapped in a blanket, she stands for a moment to sniff the air. She yawns and the blanket slips from her shoulders. Her breasts blink. Her legs shine in the failing dark.

Tanner Atkins jumps from his nest, scuttles down the beach on his hands and knees, runs like a crab to the sea. He froths at the mouth and snaps his claws. But he never catches the idiot girl. She is far away, touched by the moonlight, laughing as she swims through the cold, black water.

Chapter Twenty-Seven

The sea rolled into Rams Horn. It rose up through the soft, summer darkness, drowned the beach, floated Whelk Pier and washed across the esplanade. It sucked at the cobbles, gnawed at lampposts, strangled a cat with ropes of seaweed and thundered into the drains.

When the sea retreated, the beach was exposed – a wilderness of wet sand that stretched to the edge of the sky. Floating in this shimmering lake, caught upon rocks and shingle banks, was all the wreckage of life. Here were shoes, bones, bottles and buttons, beer crates, deckchairs, tractor wheels, window-frames, rusting drums of industrial waste, rotting shells of lobster boats.

After breakfast, when the doctor reached the esplanade, it seemed as if the whole town had collected on the beach to pick through the tidal treasure. An old man, with his boots around his neck, prised a suitcase from the sand. Beyond the pier Oswald Murdoch, the butcher, plunged through rockpools to scavenge for scraps of lost underwear. Beneath the esplanade a group of elderly women had excavated the frame of a wheelchair and were chipping at its crust of mussels. Everywhere he turned he saw people digging on the beach. Some had spades and wheelbarrows, others used nothing but their bare hands to scratch at the sand.

While he leaned on the railings a man struggled up from the beach dragging a heavy, canvas sack. He was a fat, turtle-faced man dressed in a rubber apron. When he reached the railings he paused to light a cigarette.

"Good morning," smiled the doctor, twisting slightly to stare at the sack. "What have you found?"

"Dogs' meat," grunted the man. When he kicked the sack the seams spurted mud the colour of blood.

As the doctor walked away he felt the sweat clutch his shirt. It was already hot. The sand began to belch and bubble beneath the glare of the sun. Flies hissed. The air was sweet with the stench of decay.

He was turning towards Regent Terrace when he saw two figures dancing on a narrow shingle bank a hundred yards from shore. They held each other by the wrists and danced in a circle, their heads bobbing like pigeons. He paused, shielding his eyes with his hands, squinting into the sunlight. He recognised one of the figures as Mrs Reynolds and her partner seemed to be old Charlie Bloater. Mrs Reynolds was screaming. Charlie was bleating for help.

The doctor hurried down the esplanade steps and walked towards them. When he scrambled onto the bank he sank to his ankles in shingle.

"Help!" moaned Charlie, when he saw the doctor. "I'm an old man!" He roared as Mrs Reynolds grabbed him by the ears.

"What's happening here?"

"They've stolen Polly," screamed Mrs Reynolds.

"Who?"

"The darkie," gasped Charlie as he danced. "She thinks I'm hiding that darkie sailor."

"You bastard," hissed Mrs Reynolds. She slapped him so hard that he fell down.

"Stop it," the doctor ordered, trying to catch Mrs Reynolds by the wrist.

"Where's he hiding?" she demanded.

"I haven't seen him," clicked Charlie defiantly. He sat in the shingle and pulled out his teeth, inspecting them for signs of damage.

"I'll do him a mischief," screamed Mrs Reynolds. "I swear

130

I'll do him a mischief." She struggled to escape from the doctor, twisting her body and pulling away from him.

"What's happening?" he shouted impatiently, shaking her by the shoulders. She felt so small between his hands that his fingers, buried in her sweater, seemed to squeeze her shut like a concertina.

"They've got Polly up there in the boat," she moaned. "Filthy animals!" She spat at poor old Charlie as he staggered to his feet. "They've stolen my daughter."

"I don't know anything about it," clicked Charlie, shaking his head in amazement. "I've got to think of my cabbages." And sensing his chance to escape, he slithered from the bank and hobbled off down the beach.

Mrs Reynolds burst into tears and collapsed in the doctor's arms. She buried her face in his shirt and bawled.

"Come up to the surgery," he said gently. "We'll sort it out."

She nodded but did not unwrap him.

"Can you manage?" He slipped his hand around her waist and pulled her slowly from the embrace.

"Where are your shoes?"

She pulled up her skirt and stared stupidly at her feet. "I forgot them," she whispered.

The doctor took her by the arm and led her off the beach, towards the safety of Storks Yard. It took some persuasion to get her through the door and into the house but finally she agreed to follow him. He guided her to the surgery and placed her in a chair.

"Take your time," he said. He drew a glass of water at the little porcelain handbasin and sat at the desk to watch her drink. She was trembling so much she could barely control the glass against her mouth. Snuffling, splashing, gasping for breath, she tried to tell the doctor her story.

He knew about the sailor, of course, since he had treated the giant for poisoned prawns. But he could not begin to imagine what she'd been forced to endure while the sailor had lived in the house. The language. The crazy outbursts. The constant threat of violence. He could not imagine. The sailor had disappeared. No warning. Walked out. Gone. He hadn't paid for the room but under the circumstances she didn't care about the money. She thought, at last, she was safe from him.

She paused to blow her nose, squelching into a paper handkerchief. Her mouth sagged. Her eyelashes stuck together in spikes.

"And Polly?" prompted the doctor.

"She went out yesterday afternoon and vanished," gasped Mrs Reynolds, pulling her nose with the handkerchief.

"Did she tell you where she was going?"

"No."

"Perhaps she stayed the night with friends," he suggested hopefully.

"No – I phoned everyone – she's vanished." She shook her head and the tears flew from her chin. "You can't understand – you're not a mother – when I realized what had happened – the world fell out of my bottom," she wailed.

"But what makes you think the sailor is involved?"

"He pestered my daughter," she hissed.

"You mean he made indecent suggestions?" said the doctor, nervously scratching his scalp.

"Worse!"

"Yes?" inquired the doctor.

"Oh, yes," she said.

"Can you explain what happened?"

"He tried . . . he tried to fiddle with her," she blubbered. She had twisted the paper handkerchief into long, sticky shreds that clung to her fingers like strands of dough.

"When?"

"Whenever he got the chance."

"While he was living in the house?" he asked. He searched anxiously for his fountain pen. He thought he should be writing it down.

"Yes."

"But she's a child," protested the doctor.

"That makes no difference to him," she sniffed.

"And was Polly hurt?"

"No. The silly bitch encouraged him."

132

"But why should they run away?" he asked hopelessly.

"He's wicked. He has some kind of influence over Polly. A special power," she whispered.

"What sort of power?" demanded the mystified doctor. And even as he spoke he knew that he didn't want to hear the answer for he no longer had faith in his own power to light the darkness of the world.

Mrs Reynolds crossed her legs, kicking out her skirt and exposing a thigh so pale that it seemed to hold the faint, blue shine of milk. Her feet peppered the floor with sand. "When I cleaned his room I found things," she whispered, avoiding the doctor's eye. "Disgusting, filthy things."

The doctor stared at the woman and frowned. What sort of things had she seen? Rats? Toads? Soiled underwear? Luminous rubber dildoes? Human remains in a cardboard box? Had he nursed a monster with Milk of Magnesia? Had he treated a vampire with Valium?

"And you think Polly has been taken to Charlie's boat?" he said at last.

Mrs Reynolds shook her head. "No, I just thought the old devil would be able to tell me something . . ."

"I think we should go to the police," said the doctor, placing his hands on the desk and pushing back his chair. It was simple. He would take her to the proper authorities.

"No!" she snapped. She cocked her head and glared at him.

"But they can make the proper enquiries," he explained. "They'll set your mind at rest."

"They'll fill out forms. They'll ask silly questions. They'll confuse everything."

"But they can help you," he said doubtfully.

"No, the police won't understand. They could put Polly's life in danger," she said. And she looked so wretched that, for a moment, he believed it.

"But your daughter might have had an accident. She could need urgent medical attention."

"She's been spirited away," Mrs Reynolds replied in a tired voice.

"Where?"

"I don't know. But I can feel her trying to reach me."

"You mean, you can hear her voice in your head?" asked the doctor. His eyebrows arched suspiciously.

Mrs Reynolds ignored him. She didn't need a doctor. She wanted a priest. "Mrs Clancy will help me," she said as she stood up and brushed down her skirt.

"Mrs Clancy?" The mention of her name caught him by surprise and made his ears blush.

"She has the gift – I can't explain – there's no time," said Mrs Reynolds.

And before the doctor could help himself he was chasing the tear-stained, barefoot woman through the town towards Regent Terrace.

Chapter Twenty-Eight

Mrs Clancy was sitting in the bedroom cleaning shoes. She had bullied polish into a pair of her late husband's best Oxfords and was slapping at the shine when the doorbell rang. She dropped her duster, tiptoed to the front door and peeped through the spyhole. She wasn't expecting visitors and she wouldn't speak to strangers. But, when she peered through the lens and met the anxious faces of Mrs Reynolds and the doctor, she flung back the chains.

"My poor friend, have you had an accident?" she cried in alarm, staring at Mrs Reynolds' dirty, naked feet.

Mrs Reynolds opened her mouth, shook her head and burst into tears.

"I found her on the beach," said the doctor proudly.

"Is she hurt?"

"No."

Mrs Clancy rushed them into the parlour where Mrs Reynolds threw herself on the sofa and with a great shout of despair, hid her face in the cushions.

"Don't be frightened – you're safe now," soothed Mrs Clancy as she pulled the brandy bottle from the Turkish cabinet.

The doctor, who had spent months wishing a plague on Mrs Clancy in the hope that she might visit his surgery, suddenly found himself in her own apartment. He watched, bewildered, as she knelt on the floor and tried to force the bottle of brandy through the cushions. She was wearing a white cotton dress and a string of tiny china beads. He stared at the big, voluptuous breasts, the sweep of her shoulders, the shine of the beads at her throat. He sat and gloated. He was so happy and confused that he wanted to dance.

"Has something happened to Polly?" she whispered, glancing at the doctor. Her mouth was a splash of geranium in the pale beauty of her face.

"Her daughter seems to have disappeared," the doctor said absently.

Mrs Reynolds had abandoned the cushions and was sucking at the brandy bottle. "You warned me," she moaned. "You warned me but I wouldn't listen." And she recited her story for Mrs Clancy.

"I think we should call the police," said the doctor when Mrs Reynolds had finished and returned to the comfort of the bottle. "Her daughter might have had an accident."

The two women ignored him. Mrs Reynolds poked about miserably in the folds of her skirt and pulled the battered glove puppet from a pocket. She nursed it carefully in the palm of one hand before presenting it to Mrs Clancy.

"It's Polly," whispered the clairvoyant with wide and frightened eyes.

"It's a glove," said the doctor, staring at the glove.

"It's witchcraft," said Mrs Reynolds, glaring at the doctor. He was lovely but, dear God, he was stupid.

Mrs Clancy was silent. She had learned to cast fortunes, read Tarot cards and decode palm prints, but of the malevolent forces of Beelzebub she knew nothing. A chill ran through her blood as she remembered the demons she had seen in the crystal. It was everything she had feared. She had let a jinnee leak from its bottle and now it had started to work its mischief. A stranger had come to town on the devil's business. Her friend had been attacked. A child had been snatched. How could she hope to save them?

"The magic circle," she said at last. "We must call together the magic circle. If this is the devil's work we must conduct a seance and ask the help of our friends in the spirit world."

The doctor went rigid, staring in dismay at the huge cherub as she rolled her eyes at the heavens. She was a gypsy fortune-teller! An old-fashioned table-tapper! In the heat of his dreams, through all those endless, easy seductions, he had persuaded himself that Mrs Clancy, alone among the women of Rams Horn, understood and supported him. Were they not already tied to each other by the fine and irresistible threads of fate and fancy? And now, with a few careless words, she had snipped those threads and sent him sprawling.

"I shall make all the arrangements this afternoon," Mrs Clancy announced gravely. She raised a hand to her throat and rattled the beads with her fingernails. "We'll hold the seance tonight. And I pray we're in time."

"I suggest we conduct a search," argued the doctor, slapping his knees. It was time to take command. "The cliffs. The mudflats. She might be injured."

"No," said Mrs Clancy firmly. "You must save your strength for tonight."

"Why?"

"We shall need you."

"But I'm a doctor. I can't dabble in witchcraft," he protested. He felt angry and disappointed. He began to haul himself from the chair.

"We shall not be dabbling," boomed Mrs Clancy. She had walked across the room and was standing against the window so that the sunlight shone on her shoulders and set alight her chestnut hair. Her face was in darkness and she had drawn herself up to her full height to take advantage of the effect.

"God help us, we may need a doctor," she added softly. And the sun shone through her cotton dress.

Chapter Twenty-Nine

God arrived late in Rams Horn. He waited until the Victorians had built Him a house on Beacon Hill, overlooking the town and the wild, grey water. The church is a shock of Empire Gothic and blessed in the name of St Elmo, the martyr, who had his intestines uncoiled by a windlass. The breath of the saint, in a green glass bottle, was buried under the chancel floor.

The men of Rams Horn were slow to accept their new church since, for centuries, they'd enjoyed the special privilege of burial at sea. Wedding parties would ride in a decorated wagon to the church at Upton Gabriel. And other, more ancient, ceremonies were conducted in the shelter of the woods. But they learned to live with God as their neighbour. At Harvest Festivals they brought Him fresh lobsters, mackerels, prawns and baskets of whelks. At Christmas they muffled the flagstones with straw and draped the nave with bright beards of holly.

The Tower The brick and limestone square tower is flanked by ornamented buttresses. The shingled spire has been removed.

The Chancel The walls of the chancel are dressed with Purbeck marble. Over the narrow chancel arch hangs a curious sepulchral sculpture comprising twenty terracotta skeletons in flight.

The Pulpit A local carpenter built the pulpit with oak salvaged from the wreck of *The Whistler* which ran aground in the Great Storm of 1912.

The Lectern A most unusual lectern carved as an albatross with outstretched wings. Although most lecterns take the shape of eagles, other birds are not unknown. A pelican lectern can be seen at Rockbeare near Exeter and a turkey at Boynton near Bridlington.

The Horse Brass A brass dedicated to the memory of the notorious parson, Hercules Shanks, may be found in the floor of the nave by the west door. The plate is engraved with a prancing pony.

The Windows The original windows, since destroyed, were the work of a student of William Morris. The glass in the west window depicted the seven deadly sins. Lust and Gluttony were portrayed by an unfrocked matron in the arms of a giant squid.

The church of St Elmo commands fine views across the town and surrounding countryside. In earlier times the hill on which the church stands had been a sacred beacon, a landmark in a straight ley line that stretches from the Rams Horn Barrow to Stonehenge on Salisbury Plain. The hill aligns with the monolithic pagan stone planted on the bank beyond Drizzle which, in its turn, leads the eye over the hills to the Magog giant cut in the chalk above Sixpenny Hilton. From the mouth of Magog the magic, invisible road leads directly to the earthworks at Badbury Rings, near Wimborne Minster, and through to Stonehenge.

Beacon Hill is an ancient acupuncture point in the belly of the planet, a magnetic valve, the fragment of a lost star map. On the feast of St Elmo – the second day in June 1930 and seven years after Sir Percy had disturbed the Wheel Barrow – the hill swallowed the church. The foundations sank, the tower cracked and the windows exploded like shell bursts. Now the church is closed, brambles grow in the porch, the roof has collapsed and horseshoe bats nest in the ribs of the chancel skeletons. God went to live in Drizzle.

Chapter Thirty

Mrs Clancy had spent the afternoon preparing herself for the seance. She had buttoned herself into a black silk dress that forced up her breasts, pulled back her stomach and fell, exhausted, in loose folds to her feet. She wore a gold chain, thin as a thread, around one ankle and sported a silver crucifix at her neck. The full weight of her chestnut hair spilled about her shoulders. Her mouth was painted and her fingers were crusty with rings.

In the consulting room the Chinese curtains had been drawn against the night. Sticks of incense wafted perfumed smoke across the heavy, polished table. A pair of church candles spluttered beside the door. The light from the candles flew madly about the room, touching everything and resting nowhere. It spun off the backs of chairs, ran along the bookshelves and sparked in the eyes of the dragons. It spread in bright bursts, washing against the walls, flashing on china, winking on glass, flickered, lost strength and, smouldering, retreated. It leapt and spun and danced so that the whole room seemed to tremble, a mirage of shadows and reflections.

As her guests arrived, Mrs Clancy arranged them at the table until the magic circle was complete. The two little suitors, Hazlitt and Vine, sat with the clairvoyant wedged between them. Hazlitt, the Dorchester florist, looked splendid in a pink satin waistcoat. He had pinned a living rose to his collar and sprayed himself with sweet cologne. Vine the tailor had turned out his best suit and wore a tie pin shaped like a cutlass. The two rivals pressed forward in their chairs, glaring at each other as they crowded against the object of their devotion.

Mrs Reynolds sat next to Hazlitt. Silent, sulking, she sat with her head bent and a teardrop hanging from the tip of her nose. She had spent her time making a doll in the image of the darkie sailor and had speared the testes with needles. If she couldn't catch him she hoped, at least, to slow him down.

Perched next to her was a very old and brittle lady who had been driven down from Swanage, carried up the stairs, sat down in the chair and wrapped in blankets by her chauffeur. He sat next to her now, a thin man in a grey uniform with gold buttons and tight leather boots. His face had all the dignity and charm of an undertaker and he had a nervous habit of reaching out to touch her wrist, searching for her pulse.

Next to the chauffeur sat an old man nursing a violin. He lived upstairs and, as soon as he'd heard that Mrs Clancy was planning a seance he had offered his services in the hope of being able to tempt the spirits out of the woodwork and into her perfumed lap. He had once played the part of a gypsy violinist in a Bournemouth hotel and this remote association with Romany folk lore had been enough to convince Mrs Clancy that his music might prove a potent charm in attracting ghosts. He sat, stiff as a bookend, waiting for her signal to begin the serenade.

The doctor had been squeezed between the violinist and Vine. He sat and stared at Mrs Clancy with a doubtful smile on his big, crumpled face.

Mrs Clancy smiled at each of her guests in turn and having paused long enough to be properly admired, began to explain the purpose of their meeting. A young girl had disappeared while under the influence of demonic possession. Mrs Reynolds, the mother of the child, had turned to them for help.

Mrs Reynolds squeezed several tears from her lovely eyes and allowed them to roll down her face. No one could understand the pain of a grieving mother. She would have done anything to prevent Polly from falling into the sailor's hands.

If it wasn't too late, if there was hope, she would gladly offer *herself* in exchange for her daughter's freedom. She would need time to pack a suitcase, of course, but she was ready and willing to make the sacrifice. Perhaps Mrs Clancy could make the arrangements.

It was dangerous, the clairvoyant reminded them, to trifle with the forces of darkness. But since, as members of the magic circle, they had all participated in calling up the spirits they must now feel responsible for the events that threatened to overwhelm them. Tonight she would attempt to conduct a seance to find her late husband. She believed that only the Captain would help them enter the twilight world of the walking dead and return the child to the land of the living.

"Captain Turnpike Clancy disappeared under mysterious circumstances many years ago in Southampton Water. In a few minutes I hope to summon him into our midst," she announced nervously.

"The ladies, of course, will be in no danger," said Hazlitt as he patted Mrs Reynolds' hand.

Mrs Clancy frowned in disapproval. "He was my husband," she boomed.

Hazlitt and Vine both nodded miserably and hung their heads. They began to consider their own safety.

"To help you better understand the phenomenon you will witness I feel I should give you a brief description of my late husband," Mrs Clancy announced and ran her gaze along the row of silent faces, pausing for a moment to stare at the doctor. Then she began to describe the Captain in the most extravagant terms. She laboured her audience with a detailed history of the man, recounting his generosity, his audacity and courage. Her eyes glittered with the fires of old glories. Her face flushed with passion. She described his virtues as a husband, his talents as a soldier and his reputation as a man of perfect and fastidious taste. She contrived to illustrate his qualities with short anecdotes, quotations and snatches of blank verse. She came very close to demanding that he be elected a saint.

The warmth of the room and the pulse of the candlelight

drew her audience down into a soporific trance from which only the chauffeur managed to escape by cracking his knuckles and flexing his feet inside his boots. Vine stifled a yawn. The doctor scratched his chin.

During an account of the Captain's early army service, which had started to take on the proportions of an epic ballad, the old lady fell asleep and began to sway dangerously on her chair, so that she had to be supported between Mrs Reynolds and the grey chauffeur. Hazlitt, reaching out behind Mrs Reynolds in an attempt to lend his own weight to the fragile dreamer, lost his balance and had to be rescued by Mrs Clancy.

When the audience was settled again, the clairvoyant threw out her arms and promised everyone that the Captain, once identified, would be able to answer their most personal questions, forecast the future and explain the past. This seemed to have the desired effect upon her guests. Spines stiffened, there was a general mutter of excitement and even the old lady was awake and trembling.

"Ask it about Willie," she cried. "Ask it about Willie."

There was an embarrassed silence. The chauffeur smiled thinly, slipped a long, cool hand beneath the blanket and after a few moments sobbing the ancient princess fell quiet again and closed her eyes.

Mrs Clancy nodded at the violinist. He cleared his throat, tucked the instrument under his chin and began to play a soft and mournful melody that seemed to rise and fall with the candlelight. Within moments the clairvoyant was lost to the world, her eyes closed and her mouth set loose and quivering. The audience linked hands.

"Captain," whispered Mrs Clancy. "Speak to your disciples." The candles hissed and flared.

"Captain," crooned Mrs Clancy. "Help us, we beseech thee, dear spirit, to rescue poor Polly from the gates of Hell." Around the walls the shelves creaked and ornaments rattled. Books sighed and puffed out their pages.

"What's happening?" whispered the doctor.

"She is communicating with the other world," whispered Vine helpfully.

143

"How long does it take?" the doctor demanded.

Mrs Clancy began to swell to twice her natural size. Her shoulders looked huge. Her breasts ballooned through the tight black dress until the silk stretched and the stitches squeaked.

No-one noticed the bible floating towards the table. Everyone concentrated on Mrs Clancy as she heaved and sighed and continued her interrogation of the ether. But when the book had completed its journey and began to hover above the clairvoyant's head the entire assembly gasped.

Mrs Clancy, eyes closed in concentration, knew nothing. But she sensed a sudden change in the mood of the audience. She opened one eye a fraction and squinted furtively through her lashes. Everyone was staring in horror at a space a few inches above her head. She closed her eyes tighter and began to pray beneath her breath.

"It's flying," cried Hazlitt, unable to contain himself. "A miracle. It's flying."

The bible rose to the ceiling, spun in circles and then fell to earth with a great bang and a flutter of feathering pages.

"We are your friends," called Mrs Clancy urgently. She tilted her head and stared at the ceiling. The crucifix flashed between her breasts.

The shelves rattled as a full set of encyclopedias shot from the shadows and flew, in alphabetical order, towards the magic circle.

"Willie," screamed the old lady. "Willie, behave yourself."

"Hazlitt," shouted Vine. "They're trying to kill Hazlitt." He waved his hand at his rival, hoping to direct the haunted volumes away from himself and towards the appropriate target.

"Shut up," spat Hazlitt. He clasped Mrs Reynolds's head in his hands and pressed it against his chest as if protecting a priceless glass bowl. She struggled for a moment, burst into tears and feigned a faint. The sound of her distress unsettled the old lady and the chauffeur, concerned for the safety of his charge, tried to pull the blanket over her head and wrap her into a parcel.

144

Everything in the room had begun to sprout wings. A pocket demonology whistled through the air and clipped the candles. A morocco-bound dictionary arched its spine and flapped clumsily against the curtains. The doctor couldn't believe his eyes. "I don't believe it," he muttered, again and again, until a book slapped his ear and abruptly changed his mind.

"Stay calm," shouted Mrs Clancy. "Don't frighten him."

A small hymn book sliced past her head and caught Vine square between the shoulderblades.

"He won't hurt you," wailed Mrs Clancy. "He was my husband."

But Vine had disappeared under the table. Mrs Reynolds felt him roll against her legs and screamed. Hazlitt released her head, jumped from his chair and was neatly chopped in half by a book of dreams. He capsized on the carpet, his legs kicking and his face black. Mrs Reynolds screamed again and fell upon him, shielding his head in the folds of her skirt.

"The Captain will be pleased to answer your questions," bellowed Mrs Clancy through the barrage of books.

The violinist took this as a signal from the management to change the mood of the music and flew into a brisk selection of gypsy dances.

"Polly!" bawled Mrs Reynolds. "Polly, where are you?"

A book struck the fiddler in the face, bursting an eyebrow. He shouted in pain, dropped the violin, scrambled to retrieve it, trampled on it, dissolved in tears, and fled bleeding with the instrument hidden under his coat.

Mrs Clancy tore the crucifix from her neck and stood holding it high above her head. She closed her eyes and shouted the Lord's Prayer. But it was too late. Below in the street the chauffeur was already trying to manoeuvre his priceless bundle back into the safety of the limousine. The doctor had managed to drag Mrs Reynolds from the fallen florist and was leading her away. The bombardment had ceased. No one screamed. Nothing flew against the furniture. There was silence. When the clairvoyant opened her eyes again it was just in time to see Hazlitt and Vine scuttle, hand in hand, out of the apartment and into the night, never to be seen again.

145

Chapter Thirty-One

The next morning a storm swept through Rams Horn. Rain rattled the rooftops and sizzled on the hot cobbles. The sky was the colour of mustard. When the storm lifted Sickly had gone. Mercy Peters didn't miss him until late in the afternoon. She phoned his friends and checked his usual hiding places. When he failed to appear she organised a search party to comb the cliffs and beaches. At dusk, frightened by the rumours that had spread about Polly, she went to visit Mrs Clancy.

"When did you last see him?" asked the widow suspiciously. She sat her visitor at the parlour table and watched her light a cigarette.

"Breakfast," confessed Mercy Peters nervously.

"Was there anything odd about him?"

"Well, he was a very ugly baby. He had a funny-shaped skull and no hair. He was so ugly I was ashamed of him. I used to keep the blanket over his head and say to people, no, don't disturb him, he's sleeping."

"And this morning?" said Mrs Clancy patiently.

Mercy Peters shrugged. "He had a sore throat so I told him to stay in bed," she said and snorted smoke through her nose.

"And you've looked everywhere?"

"Yes," said Mercy Peters.

"Have you asked all his friends?"

"He doesn't have many friends. I asked Vernie Stringer and he just stared at me with his mouth open. When I tried to talk to Smudger Austin he had hysterics and burst into floods of tears. I think they're both simple."

"Did you try the beach?" asked Mrs Clancy. "Did you ask the lobstermen?"

"Yes," said Mercy Peters. "They told me to come to you."

"But how can I help?" asked Mrs Clancy. She knew she was to blame for this nightmare. She had conjured up a devil, a demented pied piper who was out there now stealing children. Her parlour games had worked a magic she couldn't begin to understand. The children vanished and the mothers came to her for help. But she had locked the consulting room and she wasn't going to open it again.

"They told me you had the gift of sight," said Mercy Peters. "They told me you had special powers over missing persons."

"I'm not a lost property office," chided the clairvoyant.

"Please, he's just a little boy," begged Mercy Peters.

Mrs Clancy sighed and hung her head. It was obvious she had no special powers. She had called for the Captain and half of Hell had crawled from the woodwork. But to please the woman she took a little ivory wand from a drawer and placed it between them on the table.

While Mercy Peters sucked smoke the clairvoyant closed her eyes and felt an exquisite cloud of pain drift across her face. Her eyes ached in their sockets. She wanted the nightmare to stop, she wanted to wake up in the safety of her bed with the sunlight on the windows. She wanted her husband. She hadn't meant to hurt anyone.

When she found the courage to pick up the wand, the slender stick of ivory vibrated in her fingers. It jerked itself upright and pointed at the ceiling.

"I see a child," she said at last. "I see a child with a troubled heart. He is burdened with sorrow. Or it might be a girl," she added cautiously.

"What's he wearing?" asked Mercy Peters, her eyes as big as hen's eggs. "I couldn't find his pyjamas."

"The figure is obscured by mist. But the figure is reaching out to me, trying to speak . . ."

"He mumbles when he's frightened," warned Mercy Peters.

"Yes, he's mumbling something but I cannot . . . cannot understand . . ." She opened her eyes painfully and shook her head with a weary gesture of defeat. "It's no good . . . I can't see anything."

"Try again," encouraged Mercy Peters.

But Mrs Clancy was afraid to close her eyes, afraid of the creatures that staggered and crawled through the darkness. Her head was a plague pit, haunted by corpses. She thought she must be going mad.

"It would be easier to ask you some questions," she said, letting the wand slip through her fingers.

"Anything."

"Have you recently heard of the death of someone cherished?" the clairvoyant asked gently.

"No," said Mercy Peters, shaking her head.

"Have you been given news of a sudden illness in the family?" she asked after a pause.

"No," said Mercy Peters.

"Have you or any members of your family ever suffered from any serious illness or disability?" the widow enquired darkly.

"No."

"You have recently suffered from strange headaches, fainting fits or melancholia," insisted Mrs Clancy, picking up the wand.

"No," said Mercy Peters.

The little wand drooped.

"I've felt very tired lately," volunteered Mercy Peters, anxious to encourage the clairvoyant.

The wand perked up again.

"Have you been visited by peculiar dreams in your fatigue?"

"No," apologised Mercy Peters.

"Queer noises? Night visitors?" she asked hopefully.

But Mercy Peters could not answer. The cushions had floated from the sofa and were rolling across the wall. The furniture groaned. The air bristled with dozens of tiny, flying objects.

"Oh my God!" she muttered through her teeth. She dropped

her cigarette, jumped from the chair and began slapping at her skirt as if her clothes had been invaded by demons.

"I can't help it," whispered Mrs Clancy miserably. She could not move. Her fingers clutched the table edge. Her knuckles were white.

"Oh my God!" screamed Mercy Peters.

"Help," whispered Mrs Clancy. "Help." She had attracted a curious halo of seashells, hairpins, spoons and pencils. She stared at the halo and burst into tears.

Chapter Thirty-Two

The doctor was eating breakfast when Mrs Clancy came running for help. He answered the door with toast crumbs on his waistcoat and a cup of coffee in his hand. When he saw the clairvoyant he blushed and tried to comb his hair with his fingers, spilling coffee on his shoes.

"Have they found Polly?" he asked, as he led her into the surgery.

"No, I'm afraid it's bad news."

"Has something happened to her mother? I didn't like the look of her when I took her home. She wanted me to stay – I had trouble leaving the house . . ."

"Another child has gone missing," interrupted the clairvoyant.

"When?" He dropped the coffee cup in the basin and sat down at his desk.

"Yesterday," sighed Mrs Clancy, sitting before him. "A little boy."

"Children don't appear and disappear like toadstools in a lawn," he complained.

Mrs Clancy stared anxiously at her hands. She hadn't slept and her eyes were aching from the glare of the lamp on the desk. "You were at the seance, doctor. What did you make of it?" she asked softly.

The doctor took a deep breath and groped for compliments. "Well, there are things we can't explain . . . you have a most mysterious gift . . ." he managed to mumble.

But Mrs Clancy was shaking her head. "It was a disaster. Everything went wrong. They come to me for help but I can't control what happens. They expect me to be able to snap my fingers and open graveyards. They think I can control the dead like a troupe of dancing monkeys."

The doctor arched an eyebrow and leaned back comfortably in his chair. He hadn't expected Mrs Clancy to suffer doubts of faith. "You mustn't blame yourself," he said kindly. "I think you helped Mrs Reynolds."

"I can't help anyone. I'm the one who needs help," she sobbed. "I'm going mad."

"Nonsense," smiled the doctor. He picked a toast crumb from his waistcoat and rolled it gently between his fingers. He wanted to reach out and cradle her head in his arms, wiping the pain from her eyes with his thumbs.

"Yes," she insisted. "Yes. In another time they would have burned me as a witch."

"Now what makes you say that?" he scolded, leaning forward and folding his hands on the desk. She was wearing a loose cotton dress and glass earrings shaped like acorns. When she moved her head the acorns swung against her neck. He wanted to kick over the desk, scoop her into his arms and suck out all the guilt and misery with his mouth. Papers flying. Acorns rolling. Mrs Clancy, I love you.

"I see things," whispered the clairvoyant. "Monsters. Demons. Disgusting, horrible things. They're crawling around inside my head. I'm frightened to sleep."

"Do they talk to you?"

"No, they laugh and whisper."

"Ah," said the doctor and nodded. Were they jealous devils? Would they attack him if he tried to touch that which they possessed?

"You're a medical man. I don't expect you to believe in magic," said Mrs Clancy.

"I believe in miracles. I've seen enough of those in hospitals. Torn limbs that heal themselves. Tumours that shrink and vanish overnight. Sick men who die and come back to life," confided the doctor.

"Yes?" said Mrs Clancy hopefully.

The doctor nodded.

"I need a miracle," she whispered, playing nervously with the buttons on her dress.

"Slip off your clothes and I'll have a look at you," he said quickly, frowning, poking through the piles of paper on his desk.

"It's not a physical disorder, doctor," said Mrs Clancy doubtfully.

"I've seen men driven mad by insomnia, attacks of migraine that led to suicide," he growled. "The brain is a delicate machine. The slightest disturbance can help to unbalance it."

"Yes, my head hurts," agreed Mrs Clancy, frowning as she fingered her temples.

"And the head is connected to the spine. You'll find a gown behind the screen. Slip off your clothes and I'll have a look . . ."

Mrs Clancy stood up and walked slowly, very slowly, towards the screen. She peeked inside, drew back, hesitated, sniffed, cocked her head, stepped forward and finally disappeared from view.

The doctor held his breath and tried to listen for the soft fluttering fall of her clothes. He wiped his face with his hand. He felt hot and his ears smouldered. Somewhere a dog was barking.

"Can you manage?" he said after a few minutes.

"Yes," she said. She stepped from the shelter of the screen spinning the gown around her like a sheet. The daylight barely touched her skin. But the doctor was watching, waiting, and for one tantalising moment he caught her full, Victorian beauty, the voluptuous curve of her belly and the heavy swing of her breasts. He struck with the speed of a cobra but it was he who stood wounded, trembling, unable to move across the sun-drenched carpet to follow his prey. He had not been prepared for such size and grace, he had not expected such sensual power, he was slain by her beauty.

"Lie down," he said, gesturing towards the thin, metal bed.

Mrs Clancy gingerly clambered aboard and settled her head on the pillow. She stared quietly at the ceiling.

"Make yourself comfortable," he said as he knelt down and held her wrist. Her hand was small and plump, the knuckles dimpled and the fingers dainty.

"Have you noticed anything lately?" he said.

"Noticed anything?" she repeated. Was it not enough that a goblin menagerie fornicated on her eiderdown at night?

"Loss of appetite? Difficulty breathing?" he explained.

"I don't sleep."

"Well, let me look at you," said the doctor as he began his examination. Mrs Clancy modestly closed her eyes. Careful as a gigolo he opened the gown from shoulder to waist. Crafty as an exorcist he examined her skin for the marks of a witch. Everything about her was of imperial proportion, the gleaming cascade of chestnut hair, the shoulders mysteriously saturated with the smell of vanilla, the pope-purple nipples on those abundant breasts, and most especially the mighty pumpkin belly as it proudly pushed through the gown.

He passed his hands low over her body with the elaborate gestures of a demented somnambulist, his fingers not daring to touch her skin yet, so close, they absorbed something of its radiated heat.

"Does it hurt when I touch you . . . here?" he said, at last, his timid fingers tapping on the polished slope above her breasts.

"No," she whispered.

"Does it hurt when I touch you . . . there?" he said and slipped his hand beneath the heavy, overhanging fruit to fondle her heart with the ball of his thumb.

"No," she whispered.

"And here," as his fingers reluctantly withdrew and continued across the broad sweep of her belly.

"No," she whispered.

"And here?" he said. His hand strayed past her hips, down, down, far beyond the help of Hippocrates, the angels and God, towards the first stray brambles of hair that poked deliciously through the fold of the robe. "And here?" He closed his eyes.

153

He clenched his teeth. He tried to stop himself. But his hand continued to plunge forward on its devious errand. His fingers seized the plump pincushion of flesh and gave it a cruel squeeze.

"Oh, yes!" gasped Mrs Clancy. She winced with pain and surprise. "Yes, it hurts me there," she cried triumphantly.

The doctor sprang from the table and fell against the desk.

Mrs Clancy, blissfully ignorant of the violation she had so narrowly escaped at the hands of the madman, raised herself on her elbows and opened her eyes. "What's wrong?" She glanced at the doctor with a worried frown. He looked quite sick. He shivered. His eyes were delirious and shining. Had he discovered something so terrible that he dared not speak of it? Or was he suffering some malady of his own and bravely hoped to conceal the fact from his patients?

"Oh, I don't think it's anything serious. You mustn't worry about it," he said, struggling to compose himself. His hands were shaking and his collar was damp. He staggered along the edge of the desk, picked up a pencil and dropped it. "But I'd like to see you again," he added casually.

"When?" asked Mrs Clancy, wrapping herself safely in the robe.

The doctor shrugged. "It's not urgent. Whenever you have the time," he said, flicking through the pages of his empty diary. "Tomorrow?"

"Yes, of course," said Mrs Clancy. She was shocked. It was serious.

He nodded. "Fine. Now I wonder if you could manage a small urine sample? I'd like to make a few tests," he said and smiled with all the charm and cunning of the dangerously insane.

"I'll try."

"If you take this jug and go behind the screen . . ." he explained, giving her a little plastic beaker wrapped in a paper sleeve.

Mrs Clancy took the beaker and obediently hid behind the screen.

The exhausted doctor collapsed in his chair. He stared at

the screen with bulging, love-lorn eyes. He tried to imagine her squatting to piddle, feet spread, knees bent, hands held between her thighs, waiting for the hot squirt of water to rattle into his beaker.

When the clairvoyant returned she was dressed and holding a warm beaker of water.

"Well done," he said, stepping forward and snatching the beaker from her outstretched hand.

"What's wrong with me?" she asked again. He gave her little offering such a queer look that, she felt sure, it must betray symptoms of a ghastly disease.

"There's no cause for alarm," he said quietly.

"Can you cure it?"

"It's complicated. It requires more investigation. I'd like to examine you again," he confessed. "Properly. A full examination."

"Yes?"

"There's nothing to it. But it takes time . . ."

"I'm in your hands, doctor."

"Good. We'll start your treatment tomorrow."

"Thank you," said Mrs Clancy, smiling bravely.

When she had gone he placed the beaker on his desk and sat to admire it, as a man might admire a glass of fine wine, placing it against the light to admire its colour and strength.

He remained at his desk for the rest of the day, plotting the conquest of Mrs Clancy, widow. After many hours of tortured argument, he thought he knew the answer. He would concoct a modern love potion, an aphrodisiac, a prescription strong enough to intoxicate her brain, bewilder her eyes and set her belly boiling. He blew the dust from his textbooks and began his search for the precious elixir among the foxed and curling pages. In the agony of love, among the dark, distorting mirrors in which he groped for comfort, the idea seemed so simple, so perfectly natural, that he laughed and clapped his hands with pleasure. He would lubricate her limbs and liberate her spirit. He would find the fuel to stoke her engine until she whistled and steamed with lust.

Tomorrow they would make the furniture dance and the air sing. They would terrify ghosts, corrupt demons and make skeletons clatter in coffins.

Chapter Thirty-Three

"Fiddle Stick Stew, Fiddle Stick Stew,
Smack my arse and I'll kiss you,
Fiddle me, diddle me, Fiddle Stick Stew."

Vulgar Song

At the time Wilton Hunt was trying to dredge his fortune from
the Sheep's mud the women of Rams Horn made Fiddle Stick
stew. They saved the bones of certain fish and boiled them
down to a thin, grey glue. When the mixture had been cooking
a week they added turnip and wild garlic, honey, beans and
lobster meat.

It was said that a man who tasted the stew would fiddle a
woman until she died of fright or sang with the sweetness of a
violin. And once a man had swallowed but a spoon of it,
nothing would persuade him against carnal pursuit.

The strength of this soup was so alarming that the women
kept its knowledge a secret. But on every feast day morning
the town was woken by the stink of fish glue. Then the youngest
girls were locked in the bakery for safety while the oldest and
most feeble women left their beds and displayed themselves
from their bedroom windows, hanging their breasts from their
nightgowns. The men would be fed on soup and bread until
they grew so hot and wild that they overturned the tables and
ran shouting through the street. No man under the influence
of Fiddle Stick stew found his own wife and no woman expected

it. New contracts were made and old debts paid on such occasions. The men rooted and looted until they injured themselves or fell from exhaustion.

The rich adventurers who came to wallow in Wilton Hunt's pyramid were soon acquainted with the magic properties of the stew and more than one hungry young aristocrat fell prey to marauding fishwives. The reputation of Fiddle Stick stew spread across the country until the most notorious courtesans of London were making annual visits to the soup kitchens of Rams Horn to beg and steal the recipe.

At the height of its popularity a small measure of stew might exchange hands for ridiculous prices on the London black market and, such was the demand, gallons of sour but innocent broth were sold to unsuspecting women.

But what happened to the secret and why the women of Rams Horn have no memory of it remains a mystery.

Chapter Thirty-Four

The doctor locked the surgery and walked quickly across the yard. His search for a love potion had ended in failure. He had struggled for hours through anaemia, angina, asthma and athlete's foot; arthritis, antacid, anticoagulant, apophlegmatic and apoplexy. But where were the aphrodisiacs? The text books failed to mention them. The best medical dictionaries refused to discuss them. All the drug manufacturers, so eager to brag of their success in manipulating every other human condition, ignored them. There seemed no power on earth that could open Mrs Clancy's arms to him. And then he remembered Mrs Halibut. She claimed to sweeten dreams with comfrey leaves and repair broken hearts with onion paste. A simple love potion should tax her talents no more than a script for oatmeal soup. It was dangerous to approach the herbalist and he knew he risked the ridicule of every old woman in Rams Horn. But if she failed to possess the secret he had, at least, proved her wrong. And if she *did* have the knowledge of such an elixir – and could be persuaded to sell him a draught – he would have the power, at last, to conquer the woman who haunted him. He must consult Mrs Halibut. There was nothing else left to him. He slipped through the town and turned towards the Jamaica Road.

It was a warm evening. The sky was empty and the road obscured with a billowing shroud of pollen and dust. Along the hedgerows the honeysuckle had collapsed beneath the weight of its own perfume. The thistles had flowered and a few early blackberries hung like clots of blood on the barbed wire bushes. He walked blindly, lurching towards the sheltering twilight until at a bend a shout startled him.

The landlord and the butcher were standing in a ditch, beating at nettles with long sticks. They stood, waistdeep in undergrowth, grinning at him.

"Any sign of them?" called Big Lily White.

"Who?" asked the doctor.

"The little ones," said Oswald Murdoch.

"No," said the doctor. He pushed his hands into his pockets and strolled innocently to the side of the ditch. "Have *you* found anything?"

"No," growled the landlord and thrashed at the nettles. He was sweating. Horse-flies, fat as grapes, whistled around his ears.

"They drowned in the mud at the top of the Sheep," said Oswald Murdoch, shaking his head.

"Or that big blackie stole 'em," said the landlord. He scratched his stomach and sniffed his fingers suspiciously. He had once fought a Nigerian wrestler called the Lagos Lion and had his legs broken.

"Old Percy Wright went down in the Sheep. Years ago. I was a boy at the time," said the butcher, leaning on his stick. "He went looking for his porker. When we found him, after the war, he'd been preserved like a pickle. We fished him out of the mud and he stared at us with a horrible expression on his big, ugly face. He was a bag of wrinkles. But there was nothing wrong with him. Except he was dead."

"What happened to the pig?" asked Big Lily White, stroking his moustache.

"We found it running down the high street a couple of weeks after Percy disappeared," said Oswald. "So we ate it."

"That big blackie stole 'em," grumbled the landlord and gave the doctor a narrow stare.

The doctor glanced at his wristwatch and frowned. "I'm late," he said, returning quickly to the crown of the road.

"Do you want 'em?" shouted the landlord.

"What?" called the doctor as he hurried away.

"The bodies," bawled the butcher. "If we find the bodies we'll bring them to the surgery." An owl floated from a tree and sailed silently over the road.

It was almost dark when the doctor reached the herbalist's cottage. He crept up the garden path and tapped on the door. How would he explain himself? How could he hope to make the woman understand the delicate nature of his errand? He was a lecher, a bandit, a common thief in search of a key. His courage evaporated. How would he escape if the herbalist proved hostile or, worse, chose to laugh in his face. He brushed the hair from his eyes and tugged at his sleeves. He was busy trying to wipe his shoes against the backs of his legs when he noticed Mrs Halibut standing, watching him from the shrubbery.

"What do you want?" she demanded. She was wearing a long, linen apron and held a basket full of some unspeakable hairy root in her arms.

"I'd like to talk to you," he began nervously.

She scowled, walked to the door and turned the key in the lock. "I don't know anything. I haven't seen them," she said and slipped past him, into the safety of the cottage.

"No, it has nothing to do with the search," he said quickly, rushing forward.

She paused and waited for him to explain.

"It's a rather delicate problem," he said. "Perhaps . . ."

Mrs Halibut shrugged and led him into the chintz parlour. She took the basket away to the kitchen and removed her apron. When she returned she gestured him to sit down, settled herself in a chair, a little apart from him, and buried her hands in her lap. Had he come to accuse her of trading in poison? Had he come to try and make an arrest?

"One of my patients needs help," the doctor said with an anxious glance around the room.

Mrs Halibut blinked her green eyes and pouted at him. She was wearing some sort of rustic nightdress with little puffed sleeves and a band of antique lace at the waist. He squirmed

161

uncomfortably in his chair. She looked absurdly young and he felt immensely old.

"I can't give you her name – breach of confidence – you understand – but she needs help. Urgently. It's true that I can draw upon the full resources of modern medical science – no doubt about it – yet there are certain difficulties . . ."

"It's very hard to draw conclusions without knowing the patient," said the herbalist. "Can you tell me something of her symptoms?" It couldn't be Mrs Reynolds unless, of course, she had been stupid enough to eat the angel in mistake for a mushroom.

"Apathy. Suspicion. A stubborn reluctance to allow me the freedom to, ah, conduct an examination . . ."

"Fear?"

"Modesty."

"Is she sick?"

"No," he confessed, shaking his head and staring at the carpet.

"Then why does she need an examination? What can you hope to learn from a perfectly healthy woman?" she demanded.

"Nothing," he shrugged.

"So what do you expect to gain from it?" she inquired.

"Comfort," whispered the doctor, swallowing his tears.

Mrs Halibut stiffened in her chair. An eyebrow flickered with surprise. "The examination is for your own benefit?" she ventured.

"Yes."

"I think I'm beginning to understand," she said softly.

"If there was some herb, some extract, that might help me. A root or flower that would warm her feelings . . ."

"A love potion."

"Yes," he whispered. It wasn't quite right but it wasn't so bad. Sooner or later some old rascal would manage to seduce the clairvoyant with claret. Why should he be denied the chance to kindle her desire with a spoonful of some more subtle tincture?

"But you're a doctor. You know that love charms are no more than worthless novelties sold to the feeble and innocent," she said with a sly flutter of an eyelash. She began to preen herself, stroking her hair, twisting a soft auburn curl around one finger.

"There have been aphrodisiacs found in nature," he said anxiously. Cockatrice blood and leopard dung. The powdered bones of pharaohs. Astound me, confound me, but tell me it's true."

"Dangerous stimulants," warned Mrs Halibut. "They attack the nerves and kill the subject with excitement. And I am merely a herbalist. How can I add to your arsenal of miraculous drugs?" She smiled and threw up her hands in a gesture of defeat. Her breasts joggled coquettishly beneath the dress.

"The power of herbs . . ."

"Some people might call it superstitious nonsense . . ."

"Help me. Please help me," he begged. His eyes filled with tears and he hung his head in shame.

Mrs Halibut studied him for a long time. She inspected him meticulously, from the tips of his ears to the caps of his dusty shoes. Then she stood up, vastly amused by his embarrassment, and left the room. When she returned she was holding a little paper packet in her hand.

"Mix the powder in warm water," she said, dropping the packet carelessly into his lap.

The doctor weighed the packet in the palm of his hand. He held it beneath his nose and gave it a sniff. His face had turned luminous with excitement.

"How long should I wait?" he whispered, anxious to pocket the precious powder and be gone.

"It takes twenty-four hours to pass through the system and deposit its active ingredients."

"Twenty-four hours?" He was disappointed. "Is there nothing faster?"

"These are gentle remedies. They work with nature, not against it."

"Yes, I understand, I'm sorry."

"Mix the powder into a paste and thin it with water. It's quite tasteless."

"And the effects?"

Mrs Halibut shrugged. "You must decide for yourself how you want to exploit your advantage."

"I mean no harm," he promised.

Mrs Halibut nodded and sighed. "But remember – a woman is safe from no one while she remains under the influence."

"What do I owe you for the powder?"

"A favour," she said. A smile crept across her face. Life is hard and its comforts are small.

"A favour?"

"I am sure we can come to some arrangement," she murmured as she followed the doctor to the door.

"If there is *anything* I can do for you," he said, turning suddenly and brushing against her arm.

"I'll think of something," she said.

He slipped the packet into his pocket and hurried home through the moonlight.

Chapter Thirty-Five

As darkness fell the landlord and the butcher clambered from the ditch in Jamaica Road and made their way back to town. When they reached the high street Big Lily White said goodnight to his friend and hurried home to the Dolphin. Oswald Murdoch wrapped his shop in its iron shutters and settled down to a veal and ham pie. But the infants continued to trouble him. He thought of them stranded in the mud at the top of the Sheep, lost, cold, holding hands as they floated, face-down, in a puddle of water. Tomorrow the tide would come to collect them and the gulls would gather to pluck out their eyes. If the tide could not reach them they would sink through the softness of the mud and pickle like a pair of newly-born calves. He frowned as he picked at his pie. Perhaps, after all, they *had* been stolen and carried away in a canvas sack to be murdered and eaten as cutle. No woman or child was safe in bed until the killer had been captured. Something must be done. He brushed the crumbs from his chin and stared thoughtfully at the ceiling. If he could not recover the missing children he could, at least, help to comfort the mothers. Yes. He must not forget the women who sat alone and waited.

He arrived at the house in Lantern Street with a smoked sausage in his jacket pocket and a bottle of home-made wine in his arms. When he rang the bell something began to scuffle and slobber in the gloom beyond the door.

"Who's there?" called Mercy Peters.

"It's Oswald."

"I can't hold the dog," she shouted through the keyhole.

"Don't worry – I'm ready for him!" bellowed the butcher.

As Mercy Peters drew back the chain Old George shot between her legs and flew at the intruder's throat.

"Damn your eyes!" roared Oswald Murdoch. He swung the bottle and caught the dog beneath the chin. Old George grunted and fell into the shrubbery. The butcher trod on him.

"I'm sorry," said Mercy Peters. "I think he can smell the blood on you." She took the butcher into the kitchen and pleaded for news of her missing son. "What's happened?" she demanded. "Have you found him?"

Oswald Murdoch sat down at the table, pulled the cork from his bottle and sighed. "We have reason to believe that your son may have been stolen," he said, waving the bottle beneath his nose.

Mercy Peters said nothing. She took a pair of tumblers from a cupboard, placed them carefully down on the table and stared at them. She was wearing a long dressing-gown and a pair of silver Chinese slippers. Her red hair had been pulled from her face and tied in a knot at her neck. She stared at the tumblers as if they were some kind of conjuring trick and when she clapped her hands they might shatter into confetti and her son would rise through the tablecloth. At last, when nothing happened, she sat down and allowed the butcher to pour the wine.

"Parsnip," he announced solemnly. "It helps to soothe the nerves."

She accepted the wine without a word. It was a cloudy, yellow syrup that smelt of sugar and Sunday roast. She threw back her head and swallowed it. "I don't understand why anyone should want to kidnap him," she gasped.

"It depends on what they want in return," growled the butcher as he refilled her tumbler.

"But I don't have anything. I'm not worth a brass farthing."

"You underestimate yourself, Mrs Peters. A lovely woman . . . in the wrong hands . . ."

"I don't follow you."

166

"Favours," whispered Oswald Murdoch. He glanced furtively around the kitchen, leaned across the table and tapped his nose.

"What?" Mercy Peters stared at his nose and frowned.

The butcher winked an eye and fell triumphantly back in his chair as if everything had been explained. "There are dangerous men in the world. You read about them every week. They use the children as bait to catch the mothers. Or they break into the houses when the women are alone and . . ."

"Yes?"

Oswald Murdoch hesitated. "Interfere with them," he whispered impatiently and poked his stomach with a finger.

"I always bolt the door," protested Mercy Peters. "I'm not afraid."

"They climb in through the windows. I wouldn't be surprised if they don't drop down through the chimneys, some of them."

"I've got the dog to protect me."

"They'd poison a hamburger," snorted Oswald Murdoch. "Dogs are pigs for hamburgers."

"They wouldn't hurt a dog!"

"Some men would stop at nothing."

"Rascals," she said with a shudder and sipped quickly at her parsnip wine. He seemed to have a peculiar knowledge of burglary and assault. She tried to imagine him dangling in the bedroom chimney, his face masked by cobwebs and his apron stiff with soot.

Oswald Murdoch nodded and peered mournfully at her dressing-gown. "Once you've got them excited they're like animals." He pulled the sausage from his pocket and let it slowly roll across the table. "I'm glad I'm not a woman," he muttered as he poked his pockets in search of a penknife.

"It's not easy," whispered Mercy Peters as she watched the butcher catch the sausage and slice it.

"And a fine, attractive woman like you . . . living alone. A warm, loving woman like yourself . . ." He pushed a slice of sausage into his mouth and sucked his fingers.

Mercy Peters blushed and swept a hand across the edge of

the table, searching for crumbs. "It's getting late," she said. "Won't your wife be worried?"

"She's gone to stay with her sister in Weymouth."

"It must be a comfort to have a family," sighed Mercy Peters.

"You'd feel better," said Oswald Murdoch, licking his lips, "if you had a man in the house tonight."

Chapter Thirty-Six

That night Mrs Clancy found no sleep. When she closed her eyes the demons grew and multiplied inside her head until they seemed to steam from the very roots of her hair, hanging in the darkness above the bed. She tossed and turned and stared at the ceiling. There was a queer smell of iodine in the room. Her hands grew so heavy that she couldn't lift them from the mattress. The soles of her feet began to prickle.

At two o'clock in the morning a vase of roses started skating in circles across the polished surface of the dressing-table. The flowers exploded in fat puffs of perfume. The water foamed. The vase struck the mirror and overturned, rolled to the edge and fell to the floor. The clairvoyant pulled the bedclothes over her head and tried to pray.

Half an hour later the bed came to life, the sheets appeared to seethe around her body, the pillows sneezed feathers. She shouted to the Captain for help. She cried for the doctor. But the mattress sucked her into its springs and gobbled her buttocks.

At four o'clock the Captain's wardrobe gave a groan and the door blew apart. As she stared in terror at the open tomb one of the Captain's shirts sailed across the room, arms outstretched and tails flapping. His shoes tapdanced across the carpet.

She pressed a pillow into her face and wept. She didn't want to die alone, in bed, choked in a blizzard of dead man's laundry. Is this how it would end? Would she be found one morning, a lonely and unlovely corpse, frightened to death by her own ghosts? She had spent so many years poking into the past. Now the world fell apart in her hands like rags.

By dawn the bedroom had been turned upside down. But the poltergeist had retired exhausted. As the darkness lifted, Mrs Clancy peered through a crack in the bedclothes and surveyed the carpet. Nothing moved among the litter of clothes and bottles, spilled powders and broken glass. She staggered thankfully from the bed and took a hot bath.

At seven o'clock she was ready and waiting to return to Storks Yard. The knowledge that the doctor was there to protect her gave her courage. She trusted the doctor. He belonged to that true company of miracle-makers. Whatever was wrong, he would find some way to restring her nerves, purge her system and settle her soul at rest. But they must hurry. It was important that he perform the exorcism before she was killed or another child was snatched from its mother.

She had chosen her best silk underwear for the examination, the first time it had been worn for public exhibition, and a plain cotton wrapper that tied with a sash. She knew the doctor would not open the surgery for another couple of hours. But she didn't want to remain alone in the apartment. She went down and walked along the esplanade, turning into the empty Parade and loitering patiently in the high street. It had been such a strange and disturbing night she would not have been surprised to discover that fish had rained on the rooftops or the drains had filled with blood. But the town lay quiet and undisturbed in the early morning light. And when she reached Storks Yard she found the doctor standing to welcome her at the door.

"How do you feel this morning?" he inquired as he led her into the surgery.

"I couldn't sleep last night," she admitted. She watched him walk around his desk and arrange himself in the chair. He was most carefully shaved and dressed and she wondered if he had also found it difficult to sleep.

"It's the heat," sympathised the doctor.

"Yes, I'm sorry," apologised Mrs Clancy, who was beginning to hold herself responsible not only for the fate of the children, but also the weather, the tides and the general repair of the town.

"You need a complete rest. If you had a companion who might agree to join you on a short sea voyage . . ." he suggested.

He beamed at her with such obvious tenderness and concern that she felt a positive glow of good health. He had such a clever, confidential manner! And he *looked* like a doctor. He was tall and grey and slightly crumpled. His elbows patched with leather. A button gone from his waistcoat. She had no patience with those young scallywags fresh from medical school with their supercilious expressions and bustling self-importance. "I have no one," she said, in answer to his question. "And a woman shouldn't travel alone."

"The Mediterranean. The Indian Ocean. The South China Sea," he continued lovingly, staring at her with glazed eyes.

"No one," she repeated softly.

"Dance on the deck in the moonlight. Brush your teeth in champagne . . ." He gave a long, exhausted sigh and seemed to slip away into a dream.

"You said you wanted to examine me," she said, a little confused by the turn of the doctor's conversation and anxious to hold his attention.

"Ah, yes. Well I think we should wait until tomorrow evening," he shouted, startled awake, slapping his hands on the desk.

She was disappointed. She was wearing her best silk underwear.

"But I've made up a powder for you," he said kindly. "Take it in a little warm water before you go to bed tonight." He pulled the packet from his waistcoat and smoothed it gently between finger and thumb.

"What will it do to me?" she said, flattered that he had taken the trouble to mix a remedy himself.

"Nothing," he said suddenly, tossing the packet carelessly

onto the desk. He looked away and ruffled the pages of his diary.

"Nothing?" Mrs Clancy cocked her head and gave him a puzzled frown. Why should he prescribe a powder that was good for nothing? He knew better than to hope he could humour her with placebos. Or was it part of some darker plot to conceal the true nature of her malady?

"Nothing dramatic," he said cautiously. "It will help to calm your nerves. Help you sleep. I think you'll see everything differently tomorrow. And then we'll have another look at you." He sat back and smiled, obviously pleased with his explanation.

"Is there anything else?"

"You must trust me."

"Yes."

"The body is a wonderful machine. But the clockworks are complicated. When such a delicate machine fails it can only be restored by skilled and gentle fingers. Teased, tickled and lubricated."

"And you *can* help me?" she marvelled.

"Follow my instructions."

"I'm frightened."

"Courage," he said as he reached across the desk. "I'm not going to hurt you." And as he squeezed her hand she felt her clockworks start to chime.

Chapter Thirty-Seven

The sun had already bleached the streets when Charlie Bloater limped into Rams Horn. He was wearing an old green corduroy suit that smelt of mothballs and newspaper, and he carried a spade in his battered fist. Threatened by Mrs Reynolds and viewed with suspicion by most of the other mothers in the town, Charlie had felt obliged to volunteer himself to the manhunt. He didn't relish the prospect of digging for corpses but, since he knew the culprit to be a cannibal, he was of the opinion they were searching for bones. Children's bones. Brittle bones. Thin bones. Bones picked clean as wire coathangers.

As he hobbled down the high street he collided with Mrs Clancy stepping from Storks Yard. He struck her on the port bow and sent himself sprawling.

"Are you hurt?" the widow cried as she helped to haul him to his feet.

"No damage done," wheezed Charlie as he brushed himself down. He knew who lurked in Storks Yard and, even if he'd broken his neck, he would rather have crawled back to die in the cabbage patch than be given over to the doctor's knife. He rubbed his nose defiantly.

Mrs Clancy smiled with relief and then she noticed the spade. "Have you found something?"

Charlie shook his head. "We're searching over Anvil Cliff this morning," he clicked.

"If there's any news . . ." said Mrs Clancy.

"We'll tell you," said Charlie. "Don't worry, missus." He leaned on his spade and watched the widow as she crossed the street. She was a handsome woman and no mistake. He'd be happy to scuttle his boat for a chance to have those haunches fill his hammock. He followed her along Regent Terrace and then cut across to Pilgrim Street. When he reached the Dolphin he found the search party already assembled and waiting.

"You're late," barked Big Lily White as the party began to shuffle forward.

Charlie muttered darkly and clicked his teeth.

"We were supposed to leave at dawn," moaned the grocer. He had left his wife to open the shop but was worried she would slice her fingers into the bacon.

"I'm too old for climbing cliffs," clicked Charlie, dragging his spade.

"He's afraid the blackie will catch him," someone shouted and they all laughed to chase away their fear.

They plodded along the coast road and slowly worked their way up the great curved spine of Anvil Cliff. All morning they ferreted in cracks and crevices, whipped the grass and drummed the rocks with their walking sticks. All day they searched the high cliff path. The sun scorched their eyes and blistered their faces. The salt wind pulled and stiffened their hair. Late in the afternoon there was a lot of shouting and running in circles when the mutilated stump of a leg was found protruding through a knuckle of the turf.

"It's the boy!" groaned Big Lily White, falling to his knees.

"Dear God, he's been skinned!" heaved the grocer and went to be sick in a clump of sea pink.

"Someone fetch the mother," shouted Big Lily White, shielding the corpse with his outstretched arms.

"She won't want to see it," grumbled Charlie.

"It has to be done. She'll need to identify him," insisted the landlord.

"That's right," declared Oswald Murdoch. "I'll go and fetch her up here. She knows me." And before anyone could argue he had scrambled away down the cliff.

The search party sat down to wait beside the grave. Charlie chewed his pipe. Big Lily White chewed his fingernails. No one spoke. They sat and watched the sun sink slowly into the sea. It was almost dark when the butcher returned with Mercy Peters.

She came stumbling along the narrow path, confused, frightened, half-mad with misery. The butcher had pulled her from her bed. She was wearing a raincoat and a pair of fancy carpet slippers.

"I'm sorry," growled the landlord, leaping to his feet as the woman approached him.

"We think we've found the boy," clicked Charlie.

"Where is he?" she asked. "What happened to him?" She stared around at the circle of forlorn faces. Her chin quivered, her nostrils flared and she burst into tears.

"Don't go near it," warned the grocer. "It's horrible."

"It's not a pretty sight," confessed Big Lily White, stepping aside to let Charlie Bloater attack the earth with his spade.

The old gardener worked bravely for a few minutes but when, at last, he peeled back the turf he dropped his spade in surprise.

"It's not human!" he groaned.

The search party pressed forward and glanced fearfully into the ground. Someone whistled. Someone spat. The grocer fled back to the sea pink.

"It's a dog," said the butcher, kicking the corpse to pieces and sniffing critically at the remains.

Mercy Peters shook her head and began to laugh. It was an ugly scream of laughter that made her rattle in her raincoat, stretched her face and bared her teeth. She laughed until she cried. She laughed until she choked. She laughed until she nearly died.

"Quick!" shouted Oswald Murdoch. "She's having a fit!"

"Leave it to me," roared Big Lily White. "I know how to handle women." He threw himself at Mercy Peters and sent her sprawling with a fast cross-buttock. "All right," he growled. "Calm down." He wrapped her face in a full head chancery, locking his arms around her chin. "Stop struggling and you won't get hurt," he shouted as he squeezed her throat. But Mercy Peters had fainted beneath him. The party returned to town, angry and exhausted.

The next morning Charlie left the boat and set out alone to search the country east of the Upton Gabriel Road. From the cabbage patch he followed a footpath that ran across the shoulders of the back meadow and then plunged through a gulley towards the shade of Fiddlers Bottom.

Beyond the trees the land rose in soft, green domes towards the cliffs and the sea. But the gulley was an undergrowth, a thick and peppery jungle of bramble, bindweed and thistle. He entered the hollow like a man wading an unknown river, his arms raised against his chest and his legs kicking through the treacherous tangle. Tall banks of dandelions moulted tufts of fur that drifted into his ears and mouth. Teasels rattled like snakes. Small tortoiseshells, drugged with heat, fell from the thistles and scattered in flecks of ash at his feet.

He was soon so hot he could no longer push himself through the stale and suffocating air. On the slope of Fiddlers Bottom he lay down in a nest of long grass and rested, staring up at the rolling castles of cloud. A buzzard was sailing high, high on the summer thermals. A spider ran over his leg.

He took out his teeth and stowed them safely in his pocket, scratched his stomach and closed his eyes. The lost children would wait for him. Bones are patient. Skeletons don't walk. He thought again of Matthew Mark Luke Saint John sitting among the cabbages with a gallon of cider between his knees. They had talked that evening of Fiji, Samoa and Tonga, of the fruit that turned to wine and the fat, bare-breasted women. But, even as they had laughed, the giant must have been plotting his murders. The delicate scent of a sweet pink steak. The pop of a kidney in a driftwood fire. Did he eat everything? Did he drink the blood?

As he lay in the nest, dreaming, a breath of wind stirred the trees and made the branches groan. He shivered. The grass fluttered madly around his shoulders. He turned slowly, half-afraid to open his eyes, twisting his head to stare back along the gulley. And there, through the trench of crackling brambles, in the dusty dazzle of noon, with his mouth open to scream and his hair standing out from his head like ectoplasm, Charlie Bloater saw the ghost of Wilton Hunt, stiff as a corpse, on his hideous phantom horse. His swollen face was white as chalk and his clothes were nothing but rags. The flanks of the nag were caked in mud, foam hung from its jaws and the eyes rolled crimson in their sockets. Slow as death, the horse and rider advanced upon Charlie until they were so close he could smell the rotted leather and hear the chink of the rusting bridle. Then the nag sneezed and the spectre was gone.

Charlie scampered, shrieking, back to the Upton Gabriel Road and didn't stop running until he had reached the Dolphin at Rams Horn.

That night the sea ran with a ghostly phosphorescence. It washed the esplanade with light and turned the legs of the pier to gold. The moon crashed through a buttress of cloud and disappeared. The black earth smouldered. Charlie, inflated with best Badger beer, continued to chill the Dolphin's men with talk of the hideous Wilton Hunt. "I saw him," he clicked. "He was full of worms and rode an enormous corpse of a horse."

The old men shook their heads and poked about in their whiskers. It was a bad omen. The last time Wilton Hunt had appeared a lobsterman had gone berserk and killed his wife with a filleting knife. One old cassandra predicted a plague and another forecast a flood.

At ten o'clock the door smacked open and Tom Crow appeared, breathless and sweating. His goggles flashed. His leather coat creaked around his legs. "There's something out there," he moaned as he staggered among the crowded tables. "I think they've arrived!"

"Good God – it's Wilton Hunt," jeered Big Lily White, cracking the cap from a bottle of Guinness. He picked up a glass, glared at it, spat at it, and wiped it roughly on his sleeve. He wasn't going to be frightened by mad Tom Crow.

But the rest of the company were shocked by the sight of him. His face was the colour of a raw meat pudding. When they prised off his goggles they stared at eyes that were blind with fright.

"You look horrible," said Oswald Murdoch, as he pushed Tom into a chair. "What's happened to you?"

"Flying machines. The sky is full of flying machines," Tom whispered, peering around the sea of faces.

"You saw them?"

"I saw the landing lights over Beacon Hill. They must have come in from the south and dumped their fuel – there's a long slick of it around the pier . . ."

"How do you know?" growled Big Lily White.

"It's glowing in the dark," said Tom.

There was silence. Charlie looked bilious. Oswald Murdoch measured the distance between himself and the safety of the cellar door.

"Well, let's go out there and have a look," exploded Big Lily White, banging the counter with his fist.

"I'm not going out there again," said Tom stubbornly.

"They're *your* friends!" roared Big Lily White. "And if there's any trouble I'll be there to look after you. I can handle myself. I'm not afraid of anything."

"No, I'm not going out there," muttered Tom.

"Why?" demanded the landlord.

"They're not human," whispered Tom. Someone offered him a sip of their rum. He flicked back his head and drained the glass.

"We've got to do something," snivelled Tanner Atkins.

"Send for the doctor," said Tom. "He promised to help when the time arrived. He'll know how to approach them. He's an educated man."

"He can't do anything! He doesn't have the strength to push a thermometer up his arse!" screamed the furious landlord. "Does anyone have a shotgun? You! Bring me a shotgun."

"Fetch Mrs Clancy," called the butcher suddenly.

"Are you going to hide behind a woman's skirt?" roared the landlord. He grabbed the knife he used to slice sausage and pushed it into his belt like a dagger.

"She's a medium," retorted the butcher. "She'll understand

178

their language." He looked around the room, hoping for some flicker of approval among the dumb and flabbergasted faces.

"That's right," clicked Charlie. "And if we meet Wilton Hunt she'll know how to handle him."

"Shut up, you daft bugger!" shouted the landlord. The sausage knife slipped through his belt and speared the floor between his feet.

"I saw him – he was full of worms," clicked Charlie defiantly.

"Perhaps it's the darkie out there on the hill," said Tanner Atkins.

"I'm not afraid of darkies," growled the landlord, blowing through his moustache.

"The lights," said Tom Crow. "I saw the lights." He was mumbling like a sleepwalker, his eyes staring vacantly at the wall. He had waited a lifetime for the night when the stars fell to earth. He had plotted and preached for twenty years, studied the sky and kept the faith. And now the hour had arrived he found himself confused and angry, unable to take command.

"He's lighting bonfires," said Big Lily White. He sniffed his fingers and took a slug of Guinness for courage.

"Why?"

"Well, he might be planning to burn down the town."

"Is that right?" said Tanner Atkins.

"That's right," sniffed Big Lily White doubtfully. "I fought plenty of darkies in my time. I understand how their brains work."

"It could be a trick. And while we're up there looking for him, he'll be down here eating babies," warned an ancient mariner as he sucked the stem of his pipe.

"No," said Tom Crow, shaking his head. "There's something out there from another world." He shrugged, smiled, hid his face in his hands and wept like a child.

"Send for Mrs Clancy," clicked Charlie in horror.

"I'll go and fetch her – she knows me," volunteered the butcher. And before anyone could stop him he had pushed his way to the door and disappeared into the darkness.

Chapter Thirty-Eight

Mrs Clancy was sitting at home trying to comfort Mrs Reynolds. They sat together, drinking brandy and crunching morosely on gingernut biscuits. They both secretly believed that Polly must now be dead but they continued bravely to talk of her rescue. Mrs Reynolds snorted into a wet handkerchief and promised to give the girl a good thrashing whenever she returned. Mrs Clancy tried to smile but it wasn't easy and she felt very weary. She had taken the doctor's medicine the previous evening but it hadn't helped to soothe her nerves or limit the destructive effect she exerted upon her surroundings. The Captain's gold-tipped fountain pen was busy scribbling obscenities on the wallpaper behind the sofa. A small pot of geraniums floated anxiously across the ceiling. She was already late for her appointment at the surgery but she felt so disheartened by the doctor's failure to cure her of these creeping horrors that she couldn't be bothered to find her shoes. She intended to keep the appointment, of course, but Mrs Reynolds wouldn't stop talking and she couldn't leave her friend.

When the brandy was almost gone and they could no longer bear to think of Polly, they discussed the fate of poor Mercy Peters. She'd been told by little Smudger Austin that Vernie Stringer had interfered with her son and hidden his body in the woods. She had confronted Mrs Stringer with her suspicions and Mrs Stringer had chased her down the street with a frying pan. But when Mercy Peters caught Vernie out on the beach she'd accused him of murder and smacked his face until he'd screamed. He wriggled and swore he knew nothing. But she didn't believe him and continued smacking his face. She might have killed him and good riddance but he made such a noise that several people came to his rescue. It had taken three strong men to pull them apart and she'd bitten one of them on the nose. Vernie had run away and now he had gone missing. His mother hadn't seen him since yesterday. But nobody wanted to look for him.

Mercy Peters had seemed in such a bad condition that Mrs Reynolds had persuaded the wretched woman to stay with her until the children had been found and was, at that moment, fast asleep in the sailor's bedroom.

"I slipped some sherry into her milk," said Mrs Reynolds confidentially.

"I'm afraid she'll do herself a mischief," sighed Mrs Clancy wagging her head.

The sound of the doorbell startled them into silence. Mrs Clancy dropped her biscuit. The pot of geraniums fell from the ceiling and shattered softly on the carpet.

"Who is it?" shrieked Mrs Reynolds as they tiptoed to the door.

"Oswald Murdoch," wheezed the butcher.

"Perhaps he's been drinking," hissed Mrs Reynolds. Yes, mad with drink and come to truss them to the bed like a brace of fat hen pheasants.

Mrs Clancy unchained the door and threatened him with a poker. "What do you want?" she boomed.

"They sent me to fetch you," gasped the butcher. "We need your help." It took him several minutes to explain the purpose of his visit and when he mentioned the lights on Beacon Hill Mrs Reynolds burst into tears.

"It's Polly trying to signal for help," she wailed.

"It could be anything," argued Mrs Clancy. Monsters. Devils. Rats dressed as women. Wolves disguised as men. Anything. What could she do about it? Did they expect her to snap her fingers and conjure up an army of angels?

"They're waiting for you at the Dolphin," urged Oswald

Murdoch. It had been his own idea to collect Mrs Clancy and he was determined to take her back with him.

"I'll fetch your shoes," said Mrs Reynolds, running to the bedroom.

Twenty minutes later the search party, led by Mrs Clancy, marched from the Dolphin and made its way towards the hills behind the town. She knew it was a mistake but no longer had the strength to argue and she didn't want to be left alone.

The landlord carried the sausage knife in his belt and an oil lamp in his fist. He growled and grumbled and tried to kick Charlie Bloater but his fury only masked his fear. He had damaged some fast and violent men in his prime and he'd taken a few thrashings too, although he didn't often talk about them. But he would rather have confronted any of them, blindfolded, than have to walk down this dark street towards the jaws of death with nothing but a knife and a lantern to save him. He'd rather be crushed and thrown from the ring. He'd rather have his neck broken and his ears cauliflowered. Anything would be easier than following this mad procession. Why, they didn't even know if they were looking for man or beast, the living or the dead. He swung out his boot and caught Charlie full in the pants.

Charlie grinned. He was so heavy with beer that he staggered along the street with his head bent and his feet pointing in opposite directions. He thought they were taking him home.

Behind the landlord and Charlie, Oswald Murdoch walked beside Mrs Reynolds. He had wrapped an arm around her waist, for support, and leaned against her shoulder, for comfort. The landlord had given him a carving fork which he'd made into a bayonet by lashing it to a broomstick. Mrs Reynolds trotted beside him with her skirt flying and her eyes fixed on the black curve of the hills. Her excitement that Polly might still be alive was exceeded only by the hope that she would catch one last glimpse of Matthew Mark Luke Saint John before he was hacked to death. She barely noticed the butcher's breath on her neck.

Tom Crow walked behind them with an escort of drunks, a ragged band of fighting men, armed with bottles and sticks.

He walked with his arms stiff and the goggles pulled down over his eyes. He was walking into history.

Mrs Clancy led them reluctantly along the Drizzle road and through a hole in the hedge to the meadow at the foot of the hills. Before them the land rose in steep slabs of darkness towards a black and smouldering sky.

"Can you see anything?" called Mrs Reynolds softly.

"No," whispered the clairvoyant. She felt uncomfortably hot and her scalp prickled with sweat. It must have been the brandy. She pulled miserably at the buttons on her dress, hoping to force a draught between her breasts.

"Let's go home," growled Big Lily White. He spat in disgust and wiped his moustache. But Mrs Clancy was already stumbling up the narrow path towards the crest of the hill. The lantern had alarmed the shadows along the track so that they darted and snapped at her face. Her head hurt and there was a sour taste in her mouth.

At the top of the slope the hunting party stopped and squinted at the great bruised buttock of Beacon Hill.

"There!" hooted Tom Crow, waving a crooked finger into the darkness. "Lights!"

"That's the church," cried Mrs Reynolds and, as they stared, the shell of the broken church seemed to glow with light. Soft, demented sparks of light that trembled over the walls and tower and chased themselves in the tops of trees.

"Well, what the hell is it?" demanded Oswald Murdoch, turning around to glare at Tom Crow.

Tom shook his head.

"Stop!" hissed Big Lily White suddenly as Mrs Reynolds tried to push past him. "It could be dangerous . . ." He grabbed hold of her wrist and threatened to throw her to the ground.

"Perhaps we should come back tomorrow," suggested the butcher hopefully.

"It's too late," snapped Mrs Clancy. She had to know the truth. She snatched the lantern from the landlord and walked away, down through the gulley and over the curve of Beacon Hill as far as the cemetery wall. The smell of the Sheep drifted up through the darkness. An acid-sweet smell of warm, fermenting mud and death.

"She's mad," seethed Big Lily White. "She'll get killed out there."

But the rest of the party was already scrambling down the slope towards the lady with the lamp. They were afraid of the jumping, fairy lights but they were also afraid of the dark.

Mrs Clancy crouched beneath the wall and peeped into the burial ground. Nothing moved. An angel stood submerged in nettles, its face eaten by salt and its wings tied to the earth by strings of bindweed. The surrounding tombs had been strangled and suffocated by jungle. The clairvoyant clambered onto the wall, closed her eyes and sank, silently, into the graveyard.

"Are you all right?" Mrs Reynolds whispered breathlessly from the safety of the gate.

"Yes," whispered Mrs Clancy. She opened her eyes and groped for the lantern. "There's nothing here." And then, without warning, a shower of blue sparks flew up the wall of the ruined church.

"It's a fire!" she whispered, pushing deeper into the under-growth. A fire! She could see the trembling blades of flame. She could smell the damp and crackling wood. She crawled through a bed of nettles and there, by the light of a bonfire, she saw a narrow, naked girl, veiled in smoke, her skin smeared with ash and her hair knotted with flowers, dancing on the edge of an open tomb.

"Polly!" she shouted, scrambling forward to snatch the child. Her head was burning, her face was melting and her legs were nothing but rubbery stalks. She staggered forward, grasping the edge of the tomb for support, scratching the stone with her fingernails. She tried to throw her arms around the girl and pull her into the shelter of the nettles where Mrs Reynolds now sat shrieking. But Polly jumped back in alarm.

"We've come to take you home," cried the clairvoyant, stretching out her hands. She stared wildly around at the fire, the graves and the window sockets of the rotting church. Dear

God, she must catch the girl and pull her to safety before they were caught and dragged into the flames.

"He's mine!" screeched Polly, wild as a banshee. When the firelight flared against her ribs she looked like a skeleton. Her eyes were red with smoke and her hair was a dusty tangle of curls. "He's mine!" She sprang away and glared suspiciously at the clairvoyant.

"Who?" shouted Mrs Clancy, coughing through the gusts of smoke. Ash swirled from the edge of the fire and blew against her legs.

"I don't want to go home," screamed Polly.

"Did he tamper with you?" called Mrs Reynolds from her hiding place in the nettle bed. "Where has he gone, Polly?"

At the sound of her mother's voice Polly shrank into the grass and tried to cover herself with her arms. "You can't have him," she shouted defiantly. "He's mine."

"She's not right in the head!" bellowed the butcher as he peered over a gravestone. He shook his bayonet at the bonfire.

"I'll kill!" screamed Mrs Reynolds. "Find the bastard. I'll kill him!"

"Where has he gone, Polly?" Mrs Clancy called softly. "Please. It's important. We must know the truth."

The girl pouted and kicked thoughtfully at the grass. Then she wiped her eyes, shuffled to the edge of the open tomb and stared, sulking, into its yawning darkness.

Mrs Clancy crept around the fire and forced herself to look down through the cobwebs into the horror of the pit. She wanted to scream. She opened and closed her mouth as if she were drowning in air.

"What's happening?" yelled Mrs Reynolds in fury.

"Quick!" croaked the clairvoyant. "Quick!"

"Have you caught him?" bawled the butcher.

"Keep him covered – we're coming out," shouted Big Lily White as they all burst bravely through the nettles.

Mrs Reynolds grabbed her daughter and howled. She wrapped her arms around the child's head and pressed it hard between her breasts. "Polly, are you hurt? Can you talk about

185

it?" she sobbed as the others gathered around to gawp at the wriggling, naked girl.

"It's a boy!" clicked Charlie. He was peering into the tomb.

Oswald Murdoch ran forward and pushed Charlie away. "He's right!" he called out in astonishment. "We've found both of them." At the bottom of the pit, wrapped in a blanket covered in bread crusts, Sickly sat and blinked at the lantern light.

They turned to watch as the boy was pulled, alive and kicking, from the grave. There was an uncomfortable silence. Sickly, wearing a pair of crumpled pyjamas, stood by the fire and sneezed. The landlord quietly slipped the sausage knife back into his belt. Tom Crow stared sadly at the sky.

"It was you!" screamed Mrs Reynolds. Now she understood everything. She threw Polly off in disgust and tried to slap her face. "You kidnapped him . . ."

"We've run away!" shouted Polly. "You can't have him!" Her eyes glittered with anger. The bonfire cracked and blew sparks.

"You nasty little bitch!" screamed Mrs Reynolds. "Cover yourself."

"Leave us alone," moaned Polly. She ran into the under-growth and there was a brief scuffle as the men tried to pull her into their shirts.

"They've gone," grieved Tom Crow, staring up at the stars. "We're too late."

For a time nobody noticed Mrs Clancy as she lay, face-down, among the ashes of the fire. It was old Charlie, still bleary with beer, who found her first and he tried to prod her awake with a stick.

"What's wrong?" he complained. "Did she hurt herself?"

Mrs Reynolds turned towards the fire and screamed. The butcher and the landlord ran to the clairvoyant and rolled her gently onto her back.

"She's fainted," said the butcher as he brushed the hair from her face.

But the landlord touched her wrist. "She's dead!" he whispered and shook his head.

186

Chapter Thirty-Nine

The doctor was sitting in the silent surgery, waiting for Mrs Clancy to arrive and attack him. He was washed and shaved and waiting nervously for the widow's declaration of love.

Despite a formidable understanding of the cardiovascular system, and a good working knowledge of the central nervous system, he had no idea how the love potion would take effect. Perhaps he should have asked more questions of the herbalist. Did it work as an hypnotic or an hallucinogenic? Would she wake from a drugged sleep and fall in love with the first man she encountered? No, he thought, it would probably need to be triggered by a seductive atmosphere and suggestive conversation. A spark to light the fire.

He adjusted the lamp on his desk, tilting the light until the room was reduced to a comfortable gloom. He altered the position of the folding screens so that they opened towards the bed. He unlocked the medicine cabinet and helped himself to a glass of wine.

He felt as guilty as a thief. Yet what had he done that was so wrong? Here he had been surrounded by people who saw signs in deformed fish and giant vegetables, who could cure themselves of everything from rheumatoid arthritis to haemorrhoids and bellyache, who drank medicines brewed from gin. They had faith and the faith healed them. Now he had embraced that faith.

It was getting late. He took another glass of wine and tried to drown his disappointment. Perhaps she had grown suspicious and wouldn't come tonight? What would happen if the herbalist betrayed him? He walked aimlessly about the room, measuring the carpet in footsteps. He tried to rehearse the first few awkward moments of the consultation. Mrs Clancy, behind the screen, rolling down her stockings while he watched her in the washbasin mirror as he stood pretending to scrub his hands. A few words of reassurance when she emerged wearing the gown and was led, by the arm, to the narrow metal bed. After half a bottle of wine he was dreaming, close to sleep, with his head resting among the papers on his desk.

He woke up, startled by a tremendous shout. It was half past midnight. He leapt from the desk and groped his way through the unlit waiting room to the door. The landlord was staggering around in the yard. His shirt was torn and he was sweating like a stallion. When he saw the doctor he lunged forward and grabbed him by the shoulders.

"There's been a terrible accident!" he bellowed miserably. "She's dead! We were out on Beacon Hill and she fell down dead!"

"For God's sake, calm down and explain what happened," shouted the frightened doctor, staring into the darkness.

"It wasn't my fault," moaned Big Lily White. "I told them it wasn't any work for women." And he shook the doctor until he rattled.

At that moment the funeral procession came marching forward with the corpse of the clairvoyant held aloft on the shoulders of the strongest men. Her arms trailed loose and her dark skirts fluttered like prayer flags. Mrs Reynolds was wailing. Charlie Bloater was singing. Tom Crow was dragging a pair of dirty, bewildered children behind him.

The doctor watched the circus fill the yard and lay the corpse at his feet. And as he watched he felt the sky pushing down, the moon crushing him, the stars screaming as they rushed past his ears. He fell to his knees and cradled the widow's head in his hands. Stupid with shock, demented by the sight of that lovely, lifeless face, he bent forward and pressed his mouth against her teeth.

Mrs Clancy gasped for breath, coughed and opened her eyes. Her head hurt and she felt very cold. When she saw the doctor she gave a little groan and slipped back into her stupor.

"He's brought her back," sobbed Mrs Reynolds. She was astonished. She didn't know whether to laugh or cry.

"It's impossible," declared Tom Crow and shook his head.

"She's alive again," burbled Charlie Bloater happily and fell against the wall as the landlord tried to kick him to death.

"Do you want us to move her inside?" Oswald Murdoch asked helpfully. He pushed his way through the crowd and began to pull at Mrs Clancy's feet.

"Leave her alone!" snarled the doctor. "Haven't you done enough damage?" He turned and elbowed the butcher away.

"I was only trying to help," complained the butcher as he lay sprawled on the cobbles. He was going to jump up and defend himself but the doctor looked so fierce he decided to remain where he'd fallen and nurse his bruises.

"This woman was under medical supervision!" roared the doctor. "She was supposed to have kept an appointment here tonight. It's a miracle she survived."

"She found the children," bleated Big Lily White. "They were on the hill . . ."

"I don't care if she found the Ark!" the doctor roared. He managed to raise the clairvoyant until she was sitting propped against the door. Her shoes fell off and her mouth popped open.

"They've been living rough," explained Mrs Reynolds, who suspected that Polly was harbouring vermin. "We thought you might want to have a look at them."

"I never want to see them again!" he shouted. He hooked his hands through the widow's armpits and bounced her over the doorstep to safety.

"What shall we do with them?" called Tom Crow nervously. He held a child in each hand and they wriggled.

"Drown them!" he bellowed and slammed the door.

"We didn't know she was sick," shouted Oswald Murdoch, banging his bayonet on the door.

"I told them it wasn't woman's work," moaned Big Lily White.

But the doctor had turned the key in the door and ignored them. He stared at Mrs Clancy, more dead than alive, stretched out on the floor. There was no time to waste. He ran to fetch a pillow, tucked it beneath her head, and dragged her to the surgery by her ankles.

Her eyes fluttered, she sighed softly and her head sank lifeless on her shoulders. He called her name. He slapped her face. He pulled open her dress and pushed his head between her breasts. Her heart was feeble and her skin was cold.

"Don't die," he whispered. "I didn't mean any harm. I was desperate. Don't die. I love you." He was crying. His face was wet.

"I waited," she breathed. "They said you were drowned. But I waited." She tried to raise her head, sighed and slipped back into sleep.

"Yes," said the doctor. "Yes." He didn't know what she was talking about. He ransacked the medicine cabinet, searching for something that might help revive her again. But he couldn't risk a stimulant or emetic – he didn't know what poison the herbalist had managed to mix from her weeds. He could only wait and pray that the widow was strong enough to survive it. He lay down on the threadbare carpet and nursed her gently in his arms, wrapping a blanket around them for warmth.

At last, when he had almost given up hope, he felt her shiver and slowly come back to life. "What happened to me?" she yawned.

"You fell down," he said softly, as he tightened his embrace.

"I'm cold. I want to go home," she complained.

"You shouldn't move – you're still very weak."

"No, we must go home," she insisted. She managed to stand up and stared in confusion at her torn and dusty clothes. "I fell down," she repeated to herself as she brushed vaguely at her sleeves. "Where are my shoes?"

"You lost them," the doctor said as he helped her walk

across the room. "Don't worry, we'll look for them tomoi

"I'm very tired," she said, pushing hard again shoulder. Her hair smelt of gravestones and nettles.

He took the somnambulist by the hand and led her in empty yard.

"It's beautiful," she said, smiling at him. Her eyes open but he could not guess what fabulous, sparkling wc she saw as they walked the empty streets.

When they reached the house in Regent Terrace he prop her against the wall and fumbled in her pockets for keys.

"Is it raining?" she whispered, cocking her head at sound of the sea as it washed against the esplanade.

The doctor unlocked the apartment, turned her through t door and switched on the light.

"I kept everything," she sang as she tottered away to tl bedroom. "Nothing's changed." She lit a candle beside th bed and waited, smiling, for the doctor to appear.

As he stepped through the door his eyes were drawn to corner cabinet full of glass paperweights, a hundred fa bubbles sparkling in the candlelight. He blinked. The air in the room was spiced with perfume. The bed was huge and soft, a silk raft inflated with feathers.

"Help me with my clothes," called the clairvoyant, struggling to pull the dress over her head.

He stepped forward and pulled at the buttons and hooks. The dress came apart in his hands and he stood, astonished, as Mrs Clancy cast off her underwear and rolled naked into the bed. She closed her eyes and settled down to sleep.

The doctor stood and watched her for a few minutes and then, satisfied that she was no longer in danger, tiptoed away to hang the dress in the wardrobe. But when he snapped open the wardrobe doors he was puzzled to find heavy brogues and blunt Oxfords staring back at him. Impossible! When he lifted his face he was confronted by a man's overcoat, several suits, shirts and waistcoats. So here lay the mortal remains of Captain Turnpike Clancy! The doctor stepped carefully into the wardrobe, intrigued by the odour of leather and tweed, and measured himself against the overcoat.

191

"Where are you?" the clairvoyant called gently.

"I'm here. Don't be afraid," he whispered from the wardrobe.

"Come to bed."

"Go to sleep."

"I'm cold," she complained. "Come and warm me."

He kicked off his shoes and undressed. He stepped from the wardrobe and crept towards the bed. Sleep, Mrs Clancy, sleep and surrender yourself to the spirit of the night.

He raised his knee and pushed it slowly under the sheets. In the same moment the widow stirred and brushed her hand across her face. The doctor flinched, waiting for her to sit up and scream, lash out with her fists, seize his belly in her strong white teeth. But Mrs Clancy was silent. Her lips were parted and her breath was hot.

He pressed forward gradually, introducing the full weight of his body through the raised knee, watching the mattress sink around him. He stretched out his arms and pressed his fingers into the bed, head thrust forward, one leg bent, a sprinter crouched and ready for flight. Now he was leaning over the drowsing beauty so that he might easily reach down and kiss her throat. But he remained hanging over her pillow, afraid that she would yet revive and discover him.

Finally, unable to restrain himself for another moment, the incubus swung himself into bed. The sheets gave a slither, the mattress wheezed and he was home.

Cautiously he opened one eye. He stared at the foaming chestnut hair on the pillow beside him. A plump shoulder had risen, pale and luminous, above the sheets. He tried to stretch out and embrace his fat-thighed Circe but found himself afraid to reach out across the last few inches of darkness that separated them. He spread his fingers in a fan and slid the hand towards her rump. When she turned again she would roll upon the hand, the trap would be sprung and he would have her in his grasp. The hand lay motionless, soft fingers sprouting from the mattress, waiting to fondle where she cared to bury them.

Mrs Clancy sighed, drew her knees sharply against her belly

192